Sed might be a god, but that doesn't mean he wants to live as one. That's why he left his family years ago, and why he's not looking forward to going back. The only reason he agrees is that as the protector of kingship, he's needed to help the new king go through his coronation ceremony. Once that's over, Sed has every intention of going home.

Mery never wanted or expected to be king. But he's a descendant of the old pharaohs, and agreeing to sit on the throne means helping his family, so he doesn't hesitate. Being king isn't quite what he expected, though, and he suspects something is happening he doesn't know about.

Once Sed gets to know Mery, he knows he can't just leave as soon as the crown is on his head. Someone is plotting and trying to manipulate Mery, and Sed can't abandon him when he needs him most.

The fact that he's falling in love with Mery complicates everything.

Mery is the new king, while Sed is a god, albeit a minor one. Will Sed be able to keep him safe, or will they both lose everything they'd never thought they'd have?

Inescapable
Copyright © 2021 Catherine Lievens
ISBN: 978-1-4874-3283-6
Cover art by Angela Waters

Published by eXtasy Books Inc or
Devine Destinies, an imprint of eXtasy Books Inc

Look for us online at:
www.eXtasybooks.com or www.devinedestinies.com

INESCAPABLE
FOR THE GODS' AMUSEMENT 1

BY

CATHERINE LIEVENS

CHAPTER ONE

When Sed arrived home, Jimmy was already there. Sed smiled as he closed the apartment door and took a deep breath. The air smelled of dinner, and it made his stomach growl.

Jimmy's head appeared at the kitchen door. "Hey. I didn't expect you to be this early."

Sed toed off his shoes and dumped his backpack next to the couch. "I didn't want to be stuck in traffic, so I left early."

Jimmy stepped out of the kitchen, drying his hands. "Does that mean you used your godly powers?"

Sed grimaced—that was what he'd done. He tried not to use them often, because he'd rather live like a human, but sometimes, they came in handy.

The look on his face must have given Jimmy the answer, because he smiled. "I won't ask you what you did exactly," he said. "But I still don't understand what you have against using your powers. You're a god. You shouldn't have a problem doing what all the other gods do."

Sed walked deeper into the apartment and entered the kitchen to wash his hands. "You know I'm not like the other gods."

"I'm not saying you are. I know you'd never do anything to hurt anyone with your powers, but it doesn't mean you can't use them."

But they didn't fit in Sed's life. There was a reason he'd left the palace behind. He'd wanted a real life as a human, and he had it. He wasn't going to ruin everything just because he didn't like the commute from home to his job.

Loki was in the kitchen, his tail already wagging. He got up from the floor when Sed entered and made a beeline for him. Sed liked to think his dog was smiling at him when he showed him his teeth the way he was now. He gave him a good scratch on top of his head. "When has he last gone out?" he asked.

"Just before I started cooking. Don't listen to him if he tells you he needs to go out. We just came back."

Jimmy went back to the stove. He and Sed had a routine, so instead of sticking around watching him, Sed went to his bedroom. Jimmy usually came home earlier than he did, which meant he was in charge of most of the cooking. After they'd eaten, Sed would wash the dishes and clean up the kitchen. It was something that worked for them, and something that made him feel more human.

He wasn't human, not even a little bit, but living with his best friend and having a dog made him feel like he was. That was one of the reasons he hadn't gone back home since he'd left, and he wasn't planning to anytime soon. His family could fight amongst themselves well enough without him. They didn't need him, and he didn't need them.

By the time he was done with his shower, the food was ready on the table. He smiled at Jimmy and sat next to him, eager to get some food in his stomach. "I'm starving."

"You're always starving. That's why I try to have dinner almost ready by the time you come home."

The words made Sed smile. When he'd met Jimmy, he hadn't expected the two of them would become such good friends. He'd never had a human friend before, and he hadn't been sure how to behave. He was glad they had this kind of relationship, and he wouldn't do anything that could hurt it or Jimmy.

The TV was still on—Jimmy always watched old TV shows

when he cooked—and the family on the screen was having dinner, too. Sed didn't care much for this kind of show, but Jimmy loved them. He was staring, and he sighed heavily.

"I wish I had a family," he whispered.

Sed's chest squeezed. "Sometimes, having a family isn't that great." He knew that from experience.

Jimmy wrinkled his nose. "I don't know. I don't think your family is normal, so you wouldn't know, either."

"It might not be normal, but they're still my family, and I'm telling you, I'm way better away from them than with them." At least this way, he and his siblings weren't trying to kill each other once a day. It had driven their mother crazy, and Sed was glad to be away from that mess.

He had a good life, even though it was nothing like he'd been used to in the past millennia. Living as a human was strange for a god, but he enjoyed it, and he wasn't thinking about going back. If he really wanted drama in his life, he would rather have it here in Pittsburgh than back in Egypt.

It was a miracle no one in his family had tried to find him yet, and he knew it wouldn't last forever. He would have choice words for whoever found him, but in the meantime, he did his best to focus on the future. "How's the job?" he asked Jimmy.

Jimmy looked down at his plate as his cheeks flushed. "I, well, I got fired." He didn't add *again*, but Sed knew he was thinking it.

Sed reached over the table to quickly squeeze his best friend's hand. "Don't worry about it."

Jimmy sighed. "How can I not worry about it? I need to pay rent."

He really didn't. Sed might be trying to live as much as a human as possible, but he wasn't one. He was a god, and he was thousands of years old. That was more than enough time to accumulate an amount of money he would never be able to spend. He didn't need Jimmy to pay rent. In the beginning, he'd asked him to because they hadn't known each other. They'd grown close over the years, and while Sed hadn't suggested it yet because he didn't want Jimmy to feel like it was a hand-out, he didn't want Jimmy's money.

Sed hesitated to say that out loud. Jimmy was proud, and it made sense that he wanted to stand on his own two feet, including paying rent. Still, Sed didn't want his best friend to worry too much. This wasn't the first time Jimmy got fired, and it probably wouldn't be the last. He wasn't a bad person or anything like that, but he was distracted easily and kind of clumsy. It was one of the things Sed liked about him. He was wonderfully human, and Sed never wanted him to change.

He chose his words carefully. "You realize you don't have to worry about rent, right?"

Jimmy grimaced. "I know you don't need my money. I'm not an idiot. I don't want charity, though."

"It wouldn't be charity. You're my best friend and the only person I want in my life. If you'd let me, I'd pay for everything, and you wouldn't have to find another job."

Jimmy snorted. "And what would I do without a job? Sit on the couch all day?"

"No. You'd be able to pursue your dreams and find what you really want to do in life."

Jimmy shook his head. "There's no time for me to think about my dreams. But thank you. I appreciate what you're saying, and I know you're not going to kick me out because I skip rent one month. I just want to do this right. I *need* to do it right."

Because Jimmy's parents had told him that he would never amount to anything, and he believed them. He wanted to show them they were wrong, and he'd been working hard to make that happen. Sed could understand it. His mother had thought he would go running back home after one week

4

living as a human. He'd wanted to show her she was wrong, and he had.

He loved his life. Most gods wouldn't have enjoyed living the way he did, but he wasn't most gods. He was Sed, protector of kingship and a minor Egyptian god. He wasn't needed back at home, and he hadn't been in a long time. The era of pharaohs was over, and Sed doubted it would ever come back.

His place was in Pittsburgh, with Jimmy and Loki. It wasn't about showing his mother he could do this anymore. It was about living his life the way he wanted to, something he hadn't thought possible.

But it was, and he was doing it.

Mery was lost. He wasn't surprised, but he *was* angry. He shouldn't be lost in his own palace, for fuck's sake.

Of course, the palace hadn't been his until recently. He'd only arrived a few days ago, so it made sense that he wasn't used to living here. He was even less used to the thought of becoming the next king.

There hadn't been a pharaoh in thousands of years. Mery didn't know why the gods wanted one on the throne right now, and he didn't have anyone to ask. It wasn't like he could summon the gods and ask them questions. He wanted to, but even being the pharaoh didn't grant him that right. Instead, he had to make do with a prime minister he didn't know if he could trust and people who bowed every time they saw him. There was also his PA, but he wasn't sure he liked the guy.

He wasn't sure he liked anyone here.

Mery looked left and right down the hallway, wondering which way he should go. He was trying to go back to his rooms, and he'd insisted he could do it on his own. Clearly, he'd been wrong.

He decided to pick a direction and just wander around until he recognized something. He went right, and he tried to focus on what he was doing, but it was hard.

Everything was hard right now.

Until a few days ago, he'd been working as a farmer. It had been hard to earn enough money to help his mother and his siblings, but he'd done what he could. Then, everything had changed. Ibuki had appeared on his doorstep, telling him he was a descendant of the pharaohs and that the gods wanted him to be the next king. Mery had almost slammed the door in Ibuki's face. Some days, he thought he should have. Instead, he'd let Ibuki in and he'd listened to him, which was how he'd ended up with the man as his PA and living in the palace.

Mery had to think about his family. They didn't have to work hard to survive anymore. They didn't live in the small house they'd all shared before, and they would never go back to it. Mery's mother would never have to work in her life ever again. No matter how little Mery enjoyed this situation, he wasn't going anywhere, because he wanted his family to be safe and happy.

But he wasn't an idiot. He might have been a farmer, and he suspected Ibuki thought he was stupid, but he could see the truth. He was here because the gods were planning something, and they would no doubt use him and try to manipulate him. They weren't the only ones, either. Ibuki wouldn't hesitate to use Mery as much as he could, as would the prime minister.

And Mery was powerless to stop them.

He wasn't even king, yet. He had to go through a coronation ceremony before it was official, and while he was acting like the pharaoh, he had no idea what he was doing. That meant that Ibuki and the prime minister had much more power than they should, and while Mery wanted to stop that and do things the right way, he wasn't sure he could.

He turned a corner and smiled when he realized he recognized the place. He wasn't far from his quarters, and he couldn't wait to get there. He wanted some time on his own without anyone telling him what he was supposed to do or that what he was doing was wrong.

He walked into his rooms, relieved to finally be alone, only to freeze when he saw the woman in his bedroom. She didn't look shocked to see him, and while she did bow her head, she didn't ask him if he needed anything. That was weird, because everyone in the palace had been asking him that since he'd moved in.

"What are you doing here?" he asked.

"Providing you with clothing, your highness."

Mery blinked. "I already have clothes."

"Of course. I've always provided clothing to the king, though. I didn't think I would be able to do it again, and I'm pleased that I can."

Mery gaped. "You're a goddess." Everyone knew about the gods, but Mery had never met one. They usually stayed in their palace, wherever it was. They didn't have a reason to come down to the human world except for their own amusement, but it didn't look like this goddess was here for that.

She smiled at him. She looked to be about Mery's mother's age, but she wore it better. He supposed she'd never had to work hard the way Mery's mother had. She looked gentle, though, and he felt himself relax.

"My name is Tayet, and yes, I'm a goddess. A minor one, though, so don't start getting weird on me."

Mery wanted to tell her that no matter how minor she was, she was still a goddess, and he would no doubt get weird on her. Instead, he swallowed and tried to find something to say that wouldn't make him sound like an idiot. "So you provide the king's clothing?" he asked.

"I do." She gestured toward the wide bed. "Of course, every king has preferences. I wasn't sure what yours were, since we hadn't met yet, so I brought a bit of everything. Just tell me what you enjoy and what you want to wear, and I'll make sure you do."

Mery didn't care about clothes. He wanted answers, and even though he wasn't sure Tayet could or would want to give them, he was going to try. "Why now?" he asked.

Tayet wrinkled her nose. "Well, it's important you have the right clothing for the coronation ceremony, and while I would have come around sooner, I had things to do and prepare."

"That's not what I meant." Mery took a step closer but stayed far enough away that he wouldn't scare Tayet. The thought that he could scare a goddess was stupid, but she was the only god he'd ever met, and he didn't want to do something wrong and anger her. "Why do the gods want a king? There hasn't been one in thousands of years."

It was going to be an adjustment, both for Mery and the country. They couldn't go against the gods' requests, though. Some people had tried, and it hadn't ended well for them.

Tayet looked like she didn't want to answer, and Mery didn't expect her to. He was surprised when she did. "You're right. It's been a long time since we last had a king. Do you know what the pharaoh's job was?"

"He was the king. He governed the country."

Tayet smiled. "He did, but it wasn't his main role. The pharaoh was the gods' messenger. He's always been the one person the gods used to communicate with people. That's what we're after. It's been too long since the population has thought of us as gods. They don't respect us anymore, and I suspect that some of my family members don't like that."

She was saying a lot, yet, she wasn't saying anything.

So the gods wanted a way to communicate with humans. They didn't need Mery for that. They could as easily appear in the human world and do and say what they wanted. "So I'm only a messenger?"

"You're also the king, so you're right when you say you're supposed to govern the people. But your main role will be to help us communicate with our people. Didn't anyone explain that when they found you?"

Mery shook his head. "They only said I was a descendant from the old pharaohs and that my place was on the throne."

"They shouldn't have done it like that, but I'm not surprised. I don't have any more answers for you, unfortunately. Like I said, I'm a minor goddess, and my only role is to take care of your clothing and to guard your head."

Mery blinked, but he wasn't surprised. Minor gods, especially, often stood for something strange like guarding the king's head. He had many more questions, but he could tell Tayet wouldn't answer them, so instead of asking, he sighed and looked at the clothes on the bed. "I like that one," he said, tilting his chin.

This was part of his role, too, and while he wasn't eager to be a king, he wasn't going back on his word.

He couldn't.

Sed and Jimmy were watching TV when the window slammed open. Jimmy squeaked, but Sed was already on his feet, placing himself in front of his best friend, ready to defend him. Whatever was happening, Sed knew it wouldn't be good. He could feel it in his bones.

A rush of cold wind blew into the living room. Sed's back went ramrod straight because he knew what was happening—and who this was.

Then the wind stopped, and Qebui was standing in front of Sed. He looked the same as he had when Sed had last seen him, but then he was a god, too. They always looked the way they wanted, and Qebui usually stuck to this appearance, just like Sed did to his.

Loki barked and placed himself in front of Qebui, no doubt to protect Sed and Jimmy, who was staring with wide eyes at Qebui. Thankfully, he seemed to understand it would be better if Loki stayed away from Qebui, and he crouched by the dog, hooking a hand in his collar, and pulling him close.

Sed crossed his arms over his chest. "What are you doing here?" he asked.

Qebui looked around. "So this is where you've been hiding. I can't say I see the appeal." His gaze stopped on Jimmy. "Or maybe I do."

Sed growled. He didn't want to make things worse by acting rashly and possibly shifting into the jackal form he never used, but he needed Qebui to understand Jimmy was off limits to him. Gods didn't usually care about humans, and if Qebui gave Jimmy any kind of attention, he'd end up breaking his heart.

Qebui turned his attention back to Sed. "I expected something bigger."

"Are you here to insult where I live?"

"I'm here to talk to you."

"I have nothing to talk about with you. And don't leave through the window. There's a door, and you know how to use it." Qebui might be the god of the North winds, but it didn't mean he had to use the freaking windows.

"Uh, what's going on?" Jimmy asked.

Qebui looked at him. "Human. My name is Qebui, and I am the god of the North winds."

Qebui waited for Jimmy to say something, but Jimmy only looked confused. "Great. I'm Jimmy."

Sed almost laughed when Qebui looked even more confused than Jimmy. He was used to humans treating him with deference, just like every other god Sed knew. Jimmy wasn't like that, though, not anymore. When he'd first met Sed, he'd fallen all over himself to be reverent. Sed had wanted a room-mate and for Jimmy to act normally. It had taken a few weeks, but Jimmy realized that while Sed might be a god, he was also a person, and now, he viewed him just as that. Apparently, it meant he treated other gods the way he treated Sed, which Sed found hilarious. It would take his cousin's ego down a few notches, hopefully.

Qebui looked at Sed. "Why is he talking to me that way?"

Sed might be amused, but he wouldn't let his cousin treat Jimmy like garbage the way gods usually did with humans. "Maybe because you're invading his personal space? This is his home, not yours. You didn't even bother to knock."

"Why should I knock? I'm the god—"

"Of the North winds. I know. You still haven't told me why you're here, and I don't care. Leave through the door, please."

"That's not going to work. I need to talk to you."

Sed sighed. He'd expected this, unfortunately. "You couldn't have called?"

"I don't know how to use a phone. Besides, I missed you, and I wanted to see you."

Sed stared, trying to understand if Qebui was telling the truth or lying. He wouldn't put it past his cousin to lie to him, but Qebui didn't have a reason to as far as Sed knew.

"Can someone explain what's going on?" Jimmy asked. He was still holding Loki's collar, but the dog had stopped bark-ing.

Sed crouched next to his dog and rubbed the top of his head. "As much as I'd like for you to eat him, you can't," he told Loki.

Qebui snorted. "As if he would get anywhere near me."

Sed straightened and glared at him. "You might be my cousin, but you're a guest here. Act like one." Gods weren't used to being nice, but Sed hoped Qebui remembered how to behave decently.

"He's your cousin?" Jimmy asked.

Sed groaned. "Unfortunately. Jimmy, this is Qebui, my cousin. Well, one of them. Qebui, this is Jimmy. He's my best friend, and if you as much as look at him wrong, I'll kick your ass out of this apartment."

Qebui and Jimmy looked at each other. Sed didn't know what to expect, but thankfully, Qebui managed to keep his mouth shut. When he looked at Sed again, Sed knew he wasn't going to like whatever his cousin was about to say.

"You need to come home," Qebui said.

Sed shook his head. "I don't *need* to do anything. My place is here, and it has been for years."

"You don't understand. We need you at home."

"Why?"

"Because you're the protector of kingship, and you need to prepare the new king for his coronation ceremony."

Sed had a hard time wrapping his mind around the words. "What are you talking about?"

Qebui sat on the couch as if it belonged to him. Loki eyed him and apparently decided he liked him since he hopped onto the couch next to him and put his head down on Qebui's thigh. Qebui looked at the dog as if he'd never seen one, and maybe he hadn't.

He clearly didn't know what to do, but Jimmy was there, stroking Loki's head. "He just wants cuddles," he explained.

"Cuddles?" Qebui asked. He sounded like there could be nothing worse than for him to cuddle a dog.

They weren't here for fun, and Sed needed answers. "Qebui. Focus on what you're here to tell me. What's this about a king?" There hadn't been one in thousands of years. Sed hadn't been needed in so long that he wasn't sure he remembered how to do his job.

"What is there to explain? I thought my words made it

obvious. There's a new king, and he has to go through his coronation ceremony soon. You need to be there."

Sed glared and started pacing the room. "Why is there a new king? Who chose him?"

"He's a descendant from one of the old pharaohs. Maybe Ramses? I don't know. I wasn't listening. Anyway, Ra and the others decided that it had been too long since they had someone to act as a bridge between gods and humans. They wanted a new king, and they found one. He's already at the royal palace, probably learning whatever he has to learn to become king. I don't really care."

Sed wasn't surprised. Qebui didn't care about much except himself. "Why do the gods need a king? It doesn't make sense."

"Not to me, but then, what do I know? I'm only a minor god."

Sed was one, too, even though he was indispensable when it came to the king. He'd never thought he would be needed again. He wasn't sure he liked the thought, either. "Why are you here? Why hasn't Ra contacted me personally?"

Qebui looked at him like he was an idiot. "Do you think he would? He's Ra. No, you have to make do with me, and I hope you're not too disappointed."

Qebui wasn't wrong. Ra would never contact a minor god himself. Sed could tell he wouldn't be allowed to stay in Pittsburgh anyway. If there was to be a new king, Sed would have to be there for the coronation ceremony. Before then, he would need to explain to the new king what all of this was about.

He could only imagine how hard this was for the king. He knew nothing about the man, but he found himself feeling sorry for him. He had to go, no matter how little he wanted to.

He cleared his throat. "I have conditions."

Qebui rolled his eyes. "Let's hear them. I can't promise anything until I report to Ra, but I'm sure your mother will be more than happy to give you whatever you want."

Sed wasn't looking forward to seeing her, but he didn't want to think about that yet. "I won't obey orders. I know why I'm being called home, and that's all I'll be doing. I'm not allowing anyone to draw me back into the drama. There's a reason I left."

Qebui waved. "Next condition?"

"I want to be housed next to the king, as close as possible."

Qebui straightened. "Why? I thought you'd be staying at the palace with the rest of us. Why would you want to stay with humans?"

"Because I happen to like humans. Besides, if I have to work with the king, it won't hurt to be close to him." And Sed suspected there was something happening there, something he couldn't see yet. He would soon, and he might have to protect the king. He wasn't looking forward to this, either, but as Qebui had reminded him, he was the protector of kingship. His job was to protect the king, whoever that king was.

Mery was finally alone. He made sure the door was locked, dumped all the clothes Tayet had left him into a chair in the corner, and flopped onto his bed. He rolled to his back, enjoying the feeling of being on a cloud. He'd never slept in a bed that was this soft and comfortable, and for a moment, he wondered if the bed would be enough for him to want to stay at the palace and become king.

He sighed. He was doing this for his family, not for himself. If it were just him, he would have refused to go anywhere near the palace. He couldn't say he'd been happy working as a farmer, but life had been much easier than the one he had now.

He had so many questions, but he didn't have anyone to ask them to. He'd tried talking to Ibuki, but his PA had brushed him off, telling him that he didn't need to know those things. That didn't make sense, because if he was to be king, he had to know what it meant and how to do it, but even the prime minister wouldn't tell him what he was supposed to do. Tayet had mentioned something about a teacher arriving soon, but no one else had, and Mery wondered if someone really was going to help him make sense of all of this.

He was nervous. There were so many ways he could ruin everything that he couldn't think about it without half starting a panic attack. The fact that he didn't know who he could trust in the palace didn't help.

He wanted his mother. He wanted to spend time with his siblings and to forget everything about the crown that supposedly belonged on his head.

But he couldn't. This was the chance of a lifetime, if not for him, for his siblings and his mother. If he allowed the crown to be placed on his head, his family would never have to worry about being hungry again. His brother and sister would be able to do whatever they wanted with their life instead of toiling away under the sun. That was the only reason Mery was doing this, and he had to remember it.

No matter how much he disliked the thought of being king and the way people behaved with him now, he could get over it. He had to, not for himself, but for his family. Things would be easier if he could know for sure who wanted the best for him and who only wanted to manipulate him, but he supposed that was part of being king. He would learn soon enough, although he couldn't wait to get that teacher Tayet had mentioned.

In the meantime, he was lonely. He was so used to seeing his family every day that he felt something was missing from his life when he didn't. He didn't want to bother them or draw more attention to them than was already on them, so instead of heading toward the wing of the palace dedicated to them, he decided to stay where he was.

He rose from the bed and opened the door. Two guards were standing there, but they didn't turn to look at him. He'd been trying to make friends with them since he'd arrived, but they seemed to change all the time, and he wasn't sure he knew these two. "Hi," he said.

One of the guards continued staring ahead. The other blinked and gave him a glance.

That was it. They didn't ask what Mery wanted or if he needed anything. Mery sighed and decided to try again. "I'm Mery."

"Your highness," both the guards said.

Mery always cringed when someone called him that. "I was wondering if you wanted to come in? We could eat something."

The guard on the left slowly turned to look at Mery. "I'm sorry, your highness. We're here for your protection, and we aren't allowed to leave our post. I can call someone to fetch food if you want."

Mery sighed. "Don't bother. I'll be fine even without food. I guess I should leave you to your job."

The guards nodded and retook their position. Mery waited for a moment, but when they didn't acknowledge his presence again, he sighed and closed the door, closing himself off from the rest of the palace and the guards.

He was lonely. He supposed he should get used to it, since he was to become king, but he couldn't imagine himself doing it. He'd never been alone. He'd lived with his family all his life, and even though they all lived in the palace, they were so far away that they might as well have been in another country.

Mery didn't know how to get over that, but he would have

to. Once again, he reminded himself that he was doing this for them, to give them a better future and make them happy. *He* didn't have to be, but he wanted them to have everything they'd ever wanted.

Even if it meant sacrificing his own happiness.

CHAPTER TWO

Sed didn't want to get up today. Qebui had left late last night after answering all the questions he could. He'd agreed to talk to whoever had sent him about said conditions before coming back, and Sed had no doubt he'd do so soon, probably today.

He sighed and looked around. He didn't want to leave his apartment. He'd bought it when he'd moved to Pittsburgh, and it was the perfect place for him. He didn't like the thought of the apartment being empty, although he supposed it wouldn't be. Jimmy would be here, along with Loki, and thinking about that made Sed want to scream.

Jimmy was his family, and he didn't want to leave him behind. Taking him to Egypt would be a mess, though. It would expose Jimmy, possibly hurt him, and Sed never wanted that to happen.

His bedroom window flew open, slamming against the wall. He stayed where he was, glaring at Qebui when he appeared in the middle of the room.

"You do know there's a thing called doors, right?" he asked.

Qebui wrinkled his nose. "Why should I use doors when I can use windows? And are you wearing anything under those blankets? Because I don't want to see you naked."

Sed pushed away the blankets and got to his feet. He was wearing pajama pants and nothing else, but he wished he were naked right now so he could annoy Qebui. "Why are you here again?"

Sed opened his bedroom door and headed toward the kitchen. He didn't have to ask Qebui to follow him for his cousin to do just that. He trailed behind Sed, still looking around as if he'd never been in a human apartment.

"I talked to Khepri, who talked to Min, who talked to—"

"I don't care who you talked to. I just want to know if my conditions were accepted." Sed needed coffee, especially since he was talking with his cousin. Thankfully, Jimmy was always the first to get up, and he made sure Sed had enough coffee to wake up fully.

Sed fixed himself a cup and took a sip, closing his eyes in pleasure. When he opened them, Qebui was staring at him. "What?" Sed asked.

Qebui shook his head. "Nothing. All of your conditions were agreed on. You'll be staying in the suite next to the king's, and you don't have to come to the celestial palace if you don't want to. Your mother won't be happy with that bit, though."

"I don't really care what she thinks."

"You know she'll find you, even if you hide in the human palace."

"And I'll face her if I have to." Not one second sooner. Sed hadn't been to the celestial palace the gods shared for decades. He had no intention of visiting anytime soon, not even now that he was going to Egypt. He would be fine in the human palace. He'd never been interested in luxury or anything like that. He wouldn't be living in a human apartment otherwise.

"Ra also agreed to have you bring your human along."

Qebui said it just as Jimmy walked into the kitchen. His eyes went wide, and he looked at Sed. "You're taking me with you?"

Sed was tempted to throw his coffee at his cousin's face. "I shouldn't."

Jimmy's smile fell. "You'll be busy, and you don't need me to bother you."

"You wouldn't be bothering me. I'm just not sure it's the right place for you. You don't know my family, and we have no idea what we'll find when we get there."

Jimmy stood up straighter. "So? You don't have to worry about me."

But Sed *was* worried. He was also worried about Jimmy being angry at him, and he wasn't sure what to do. Jimmy was an adult, and he could make his own decisions, but he had no idea what things would be like once they got to the palace. Sed didn't, either, but at least, he was a god.

He couldn't say no to Jimmy. He'd never been able to, and this time wasn't any different. "You'll be staying with me, and we're taking Loki."

Qebui spluttered. "Who's Loki?"

"My dog."

"You named him after a god in another pantheon?"

"*I* named him," Jimmy said. "I didn't realize I shouldn't name him that."

"You're fine," Sed said as he glared at his cousin, silently daring him to say anything else about it.

Thankfully, Qebui didn't. "Well, I hope you're ready. We have to head out as soon as possible. The king has been on his own long enough."

There was something in Qebui's tone that made Sed worry. Something was going on, and while Qebui hadn't said anything about it, Sed knew he would find out soon enough.

It took a few hours for him and Jimmy to be ready to leave. He could come back anytime he wanted, since he was a god so it wouldn't be hard for him, but he was sorry to leave his apartment, even if it was only temporary. He would miss this place. He would also miss his job, and that, he wouldn't get back as easily as his apartment, since he'd had to quit. He might be gone only for a while, but he didn't know how long.

"Ready?" Qebui asked. He sounded impatient.

"Already missing the celestial palace? You can go back. I know where I'm going."

Qebui shook his head. "I'm coming with you."

And that was that. Sed hauled Loki into his arms, took one of Jimmy's hands, and whisked all of them but Qebui away to the human palace.

The last time he'd been here, it had looked nothing like this. It was similar enough, but it had been modernized, and everywhere Sed looked, things were different. What wasn't different were the guards. They were staring, but thankfully, they didn't attack. Sed didn't want to kick their asses, but he would if he had to.

"You could have waited for me," Qebui bitched when he appeared next to Sed, making the curtains fly around.

The guards seemed to know Qebui, and they bowed.

Sed rolled his eyes. He put Loki down, handed his leash to Jimmy, and grabbed their bags. "Where am I staying?"

"I'll show you," Qebui said. He didn't tell the guards who Sed was, but then Sed supposed it was obvious enough that he was a god.

As Sed and Jimmy were following Qebui down the many hallways, Jimmy's eyes were so wide Sed was almost worried they would pop out of his skull. He seemed to be trying to take everything in at once, but that wasn't possible. It wasn't even for Sed, who'd been here before, albeit a long time ago.

"This is incredible," Jimmy breathed out.

"You should see the celestial palace," Qebui answered. "Of course, you'll never see it since you're human. It's much better than this one."

Sed resisted the urge to roll his eyes. He was glad when they reached a door and Qebui pushed it open, stepping to the side so Sed and Jimmy could walk in.

The suite was more extensive than Sed's apartment in Pittsburgh. He let Jimmy and Loki explore while he turned to his cousin. "Are you going back to the palace?"

"I was planning on sticking around for a bit."

Just then, they heard a voice calling for Sed. "Where are you?" a woman asked from one of the back rooms in the suite.

Qebui and Sed looked at each other. Qebui disappeared as if he'd never been there, and Sed swore. "Coward," he whispered as his mother barged into the sitting room he was standing in.

She opened her arms. "There you are. I was wondering if Qebui was lying about you coming back."

Sed hugged her because he was expected to, and all right, maybe because he missed her a bit. "You look beautiful," he told his mother.

"As always." She looked around. "Are you sure you want to stay here? You would be much more comfortable in the celestial palace."

Sed was about to tell her he was perfectly fine where he was when Loki ran into the sitting room, almost slamming against his mother's legs. She screamed, pointing at the dog. "What is that?"

Jimmy ran in after Loki. His cheeks were red, and he tried to catch the dog. "Sorry. I didn't realize you had company," he told Sed.

Sed's mother looked at him. "What's the meaning of this?"

Sed sighed. "Mother, this is Jimmy. He's my best friend, and he'll be staying with me here at the palace. Jimmy, this is my mother, Satet." This wasn't going the way Sed hoped it would go, but he supposed it could have gone much worse.

He just wasn't sure how as he listened to his mother screech.

Mery was meeting his teacher today, and he still didn't know what it meant or who the guy was. He supposed he should feel lucky that at least something was happening. Maybe his teacher would be able to tell him what he was supposed to do and how the coronation ceremony worked. Mery didn't want to make mistakes, and he wasn't sure he could afford to. He was the pharaoh, chosen by the gods as their messenger, himself a god on earth from the little Mery knew of history—although the thought made him want to laugh. He had to be as perfect as possible, and he didn't know if he could be.

He stared at the throne room doors. They were closed, but he knew two guards stood by them outside. Mery was alone inside, and he was supposed to work, but he couldn't stay still. He was too nervous. He'd been walking back and forth between his office and the throne room for the past hour, but nothing he did was enough to distract him from what was about to happen.

He huffed and turned around to head back to his office, but he paused once he got there. He knew he wouldn't be able to sit down and work. He also didn't want to continue pacing and working himself up when he had no idea what was about to happen.

Instead of sitting behind his desk, he moved toward the door that led to the gardens. He'd been exploring since he'd arrived at the palace, so he knew how to get out of his office without anyone noticing. Guards were walking around the gardens, but Mery could sneak out and get to the private garden outside of his bedroom without anyone seeing him.

So he did.

By the time he got there, his heart was racing because he didn't want to be found, but he was also exhilarated. He should be working, since he was the next king and he was already viewed as one, but he just couldn't focus today. He'd rather spend time in his favorite place in the palace.

There were no guards here. He'd given that order when he'd arrived at the palace, and even though Ibuki had protested, that was one thing Mery wasn't giving in on. There were guards everywhere, every step he took. He wanted at least his bedroom and the gardens to be private.

He sat heavily on a stone bench and took a deep breath. The air smelled sweet and floral, and flowers and plants surrounded him. It was almost like being back home, although he'd never had a garden there. He'd been a farmer, more used to dealing with vegetables and grains than decorative plans. He still felt better here than he did anywhere else in the palace.

It was peaceful. It was the one place Mery could run to when he needed to be alone, or at least, he thought so until he heard someone walking down the path toward him. He sighed and opened his eyes after taking one last deep breath. It was probably Ibuki with more work for him or maybe wanting to berate him for leaving his office. It wouldn't be the first time he did it, but it wouldn't stop Mery from leaving when he felt he needed to.

But it wasn't Ibuki that appeared between two rose bushes. This man was much taller than Mery's PA, and he looked nothing like him. Ibuki had the kind of body that betrayed his sedentary job. This guy was nothing like that. He wasn't just taller—his shoulders were broader, while his waist was much smaller.

Mery's mouth went dry. He wanted to look away, but he couldn't. He was mesmerized by this man—by the long black hair that fell down his back, the dark eyes that had now seen him and were staring. Mery tried to swallow and say something, act like the king he was supposed to be, but not one word would pass his lips.

He'd always known he liked men. He'd never told anyone because he hadn't wanted to hurt his mother and his family.

He didn't know how they would react, and he hadn't intended to find out. Besides, as the next king, he was supposed to marry a woman and have children. He had to have an heir, someone who would one day take his place on the throne, no matter how little he wanted to do it.

But watching this man made him want to say no to all of that.

Hoping he wasn't making himself look stupid, he sat up straighter and cleared his throat. "Who are you? What are you doing here?" After all, these were private gardens, and a stranger shouldn't be able to walk in without anyone stopping him.

The man didn't look worried. Instead, he smiled. "You're Meryatum?"

Mery grimaced. "Whoever you are, you can call me Mery."

The man stared for a moment before nodding. "All right. Mery, then. My name is Sed."

Mery knew he'd read that name somewhere, but he couldn't remember where. He had to look lost because Sed chuckled.

"I am the protector of kingship," he explained.

That was when Mery realized Sed was a god. He shot to his feet, his heart racing. He'd been supposed to meet Sed in his office or in the throne room. Instead, they were in the garden, and he'd just asked a god to call him Mery. "I apologize."

Sed frowned. "What are you apologizing for?"

"We should have met in my office."

Sed waved Mery's words away and sat on the bench. "I don't know about you, but I'd rather talk here than in your office. But if you want to go, we can."

Mery could only stare. He'd only met a few gods, and none of them had been anything like he'd imagined. When Ibuki had told him about his teacher, he hadn't even known it would be a god. He'd imagined an older man, someone who

25

would insist on following all the traditions. Instead, Sed looked like he was barely older than Mery.

Of course, it was an illusion. Sed was a god, which meant he was thousands of years old. Mery could only imagine what that was like, but now wasn't the time to think about it. Sed was here for a reason — to tell Mery what was going to happen and what he was supposed to do during the coronation ceremony.

Sed was still staring, and Mery sat back down.

"What did you do before you agreed to become king?" Sed asked.

It wasn't what Mery had expected, but he was more than happy to talk about that rather than about his duties. "I was a farmer."

"What happened?"

"Nothing much. One day a man knocked on my door. He told me I was a descendant of the pharaohs and that the gods had decided I should be king. He brought me here, along with my family."

"I didn't know you had a family."

"They're who I'm doing this for."

Sed continued staring. "You wouldn't have otherwise?"

It was dangerous to admit it, especially to someone who was supposed to teach him how to be king. But if they were going to have a close relationship, Mery needed to be honest. He wasn't sure he could trust Sed, but he also wasn't sure he shouldn't trust him. "I wouldn't have," he confirmed. "But this was the best way to make sure my mother and my siblings had everything they could want in life. This way, they'll never be hungry again. They'll never wonder if we have enough water to last for the summer."

"I see," Sed murmured.

Mery wasn't sure what he did. "I know this is probably going to be a disaster. I might have agreed to it, but I have no idea what to do." He probably shouldn't be admitting that either, but for some reason, he felt like he could trust the god.

Hopefully, he wouldn't be proven wrong. He had no allies in the palace, not even the people who were supposed to be on his side. He didn't want to bring his family into this, and he'd been yearning for friends since he'd arrived.

Sed was a god, it was doubtful they'd ever be friends, but maybe they could be friendly. Maybe he could be on Mery's side.

Mery was pretty sure he would be the only one.

Mery was nothing like Sed had expected. He'd thought he would find an arrogant man, someone who thought everyone else was beneath him. Maybe Mery did feel that way. Sed was a god, which meant that Mery would always come under him, no matter how high up he was.

But Sed didn't think that was the case. The way Mery talked about his family made Sed believe Mery *was* doing this for them and not because he wanted power or to be rich. Sed shouldn't have arrived here already thinking he knew the king, but he had. He'd met enough of them in the past to know what to expect.

He hadn't known to expect Mery.

Mery was just a scared young man who was trying to do the best for his family. Qebui hadn't given Sed a lot of information, since he'd disappeared as soon as Sed's mother had arrived, but Mery couldn't be more than twenty-five years old, if even that. Others had become pharaoh younger than him, but usually that was a disaster. They did it because they didn't have a choice, and neither did Mery.

Sed had no doubt that if Mery had said no, someone would have found a way to force him to accept. They could probably have found other descendants of the pharaohs, though, so why Mery in particular? There had to be a reason he was the one who'd been chosen to become king, and since Sed didn't know him yet, he couldn't see it.

He had no doubt Mery was being manipulated, but he couldn't see why. He also couldn't see who, but that was easy enough to fix. He just had to spend time with Mery and watch the people around him. No one would tell him to leave, since he was a god, and this was one of the few times he was happy that was the case.

"I suppose we should get to work," Mery said.

"If you don't mind, I'd rather stay here and talk to you for a bit. We don't have a lot of time before your coronation ceremony, but I'd like to get to know you."

Mery's eyes widened. "Is that how it works?"

Sed didn't want to lie, but he also didn't want Mery to think he was weird. Maybe Mery already thought that. He'd been taken from his home and told he was to be the messenger for the gods. If it had happened to Sed, he wouldn't be happy with any of them. "It's been a long time since I last had to do this," Sed explained. "I usually knew more about the next king than I do about you."

Mery seemed to relax. "What do you want to know?"

"Start by telling me who came to your door to tell you that you were to be the next king."

Mery frowned, but he answered. "It was my personal assistant, Ibuki. He said the prime minister sent him."

But who had told the prime minister he was supposed to find the next king? Qebui hadn't even been able to tell Sed that, and Sed had to find out. He also had to find out how much the prime minister was losing through this. He'd been the one in charge until the gods intervened. Now, he was supposed to take a step back and let Mery make the decisions for the country. Most people wouldn't have liked that, but Sed didn't know the prime minister. He couldn't judge the man yet. He was going to keep an eye on him and Ibuki. It wouldn't be the first time a personal assistant betrayed a pharaoh.

"And they convinced you to agree to this," Sed said.

"It took a while, and I only agreed when they promised my family could come with me. They said it wouldn't be proper for them to continue living in our old house and working as farmers."

That might be true, but Sed could tell they'd used Mery's family to manipulate him into accepting. He still wasn't sure what was going on, but he didn't like what he was hearing.

Even though that had been the case for thousands of years, no one should be forced to become king. Sed had seen from up close how much damage this kind of thing could create, and he hoped Mery would be strong enough to withstand the stress and work. He might not know him yet, but even though they'd only talked for a few minutes, he already liked the man.

"What about you?" Mery asked, his tone hesitant. "Have you always lived in the gods' palace?"

Sed was surprised that Mery was asking him about his life, although maybe he shouldn't be. Humans tended to be fascinated by the gods. Mery was more relaxed than most humans usually were. "I lived there for thousands of years, but I moved away decades ago."

Mery's eyes widened. "I didn't know that was possible. Where do you live?"

"In the United States."

"I've never left the country."

And he probably never would. Whoever was manipulating him wouldn't want him out of their sight. The *gods* wouldn't want him out of their sight, although that would make it easier to travel if Mery had to. It wasn't something to think about right now, though. "I wasn't planning on coming back, but then I didn't think there would ever be another king."

"Sorry to bother you," Mery said.

There was humor in his voice, and Sed found himself smiling at him. He liked him, and he hoped things would end up okay. It was too easy to remember the kings who had been assassinated, and Sed didn't want that to happen to Mery. "It's not a bother, although I'll admit I wasn't looking forward to leaving my home. That has nothing to do with you, though."

"What does it have to do with?"

"Being a god isn't always pleasant. My family is big, and we don't get along most of the time. I'd had enough of the drama and the fighting, and I went away. I wanted to be able to live my life the way I decided."

Mery slowly nodded. "You were lucky, then."

Sed's chest squeezed. Mery wasn't allowed to live his life the way he wanted. He had to follow the protocols, the traditions, and a heavy weight had settled on his shoulders when he'd agreed to be king. Sed couldn't criticize him for saying yes. He'd wanted to do the best for his family, and even Sed couldn't deny this was probably the only way to do it. Mery clearly didn't like it, and Sed found himself wanting to help him.

"I was," he confirmed. "And I realize that now that you've agreed to do this, you can't go back on your word. It doesn't mean everything is bad, though."

"I didn't say things were bad."

"But you said you didn't know what you're doing."

"That's because I don't. When I agreed to be king, I was brought here. They gave me new clothes, food, and they sat me behind my desk in the office and told me to get to work. The problem is, I'm still not sure what my job is. I'm a messenger for the gods, yet so far, none of you have given me a message to refer to anyone. As king, I'm supposed to be in charge of the country, but things were working fine the way they were before I arrived. The prime minister still has everything in hand, and he's reluctant to allow me to do anything."

"No matter how reluctant, you're the king, and he should allow you to do your job."

Mery sighed. "Maybe, but I understand why he won't. I wouldn't know where to begin if I had to do his job."

"Then he should be teaching you."

Mery looked at Sed. "Like you're going to teach me what to do as a messenger of the gods?"

Sed had been reluctant to do it, and he still was, but now that he'd met Mery, he would do everything he could to help him. "I will. And I can tell you about the past kings and their lives. I know it probably doesn't mean much to you, but I promise I'll help you as much as I can."

The problem was that without knowing what was happening, there was little Sed could do for Mery.

Mery wasn't sure what to make of Sed's promise. It didn't sound like a godly thing to say, but then Sed hadn't struck Mery as a god. Even now, as he looked at the man, he didn't look like one.

Sed was wearing jeans and a t-shirt. The day was hot, but it didn't seem to bother Sed, who wasn't sweating even a little bit. He was barefoot, and Mery had been doing his best not to stare at his feet. Who knew he could find feet attractive? Because he did in this case. Sed's feet were long and a bit bony but elegant.

Mery swallowed and looked up at Sed. His hair was moving slightly in the breeze, and he kept pushing strands away from his face. He looked utterly human and like a man Mery could grow to love if it was at all possible.

But it wasn't, and Mery had to remember that. He also had

to remember that even though he looked human, Sed was a god. So far, the gods Mery had met had ranged from being sweet like Tayet to being a bit snooty like Qebui. Sed was neither of those things, but he was nice. Mery liked him, already more than he should.

What had he gotten himself into? Whatever it was, he couldn't back down anymore. He'd agreed to be king, and that was what he was going to be. There was no way out, no matter how much he wished for one.

"I'm sure you have a lot of questions," Sed continued.

"I don't even know where to start," Mery admitted. "I've tried asking those questions to Ibuki, but he always brushes me off. He keeps saying you'll answer every question I have, and I hope that will be the case."

"I suppose it depends on the kind of questions you ask."

Mery had a lot of them, and not one had anything to do with being a king. He wanted to know more about Sed's life in the United States. He still couldn't quite wrap his mind around the fact that a god had willingly left the palace the gods lived in to move to another country where those gods weren't revered.

But that wasn't why Sed was here. Mery had to do what he'd agreed to do and what people expected from him, and that was being a good king. That meant focusing on the coronation ceremony, then on guiding the country. He hoped Sed would be able to help with both those things, but if that wasn't the case, that was okay. It wasn't Sed's job to teach Mery how to be king, after all. He was a protector of kingship, and he would be there during the coronation ceremony, but after that, his work would be done. He would eventually leave and go back to the States, and Mery would be left behind. Mery wasn't looking forward to it, but it was his destiny and what he'd agreed to. Nothing he could do would get him out of this.

Sed got to his feet. "I know I told you a lot of things that you have to wrap your mind around. We can start working together tomorrow, if that's okay with you."

Mery didn't want him to leave, but he nodded. "It is. Thank you for coming and for agreeing to help."

Sed's smile was gentle. "I couldn't say no, and now I'm glad I couldn't. I'm sorry you were dragged into this, Mery. You didn't want it, and now, you're stuck."

"I wouldn't have agreed to do this if I didn't want it." Mery didn't want the gods to be offended by his lack of enthusiasm at being their messenger on earth.

Sed shook his head. "That's not what I meant. You agreed because you were trying to do the best for your family. I can respect that. It doesn't make it easier for you to deal with, though. I'll try to help you as much as I can. I'm just a minor god, so there's only so much I can do."

"I'm sure it will be more than enough."

"I hope it will be." Sed didn't say anything else after that. He looked worried. Mery wanted to ask why, but he didn't. Sed didn't owe him an answer. He was here to teach Mery about being king, and that was all. Mery would have to find another way to get all the information he wanted and needed.

He stayed in the garden, thinking about Sed's words. It was true that the prime minister was the one who should be teaching Mery. Mery truly did understand why the man wasn't, but he wasn't sure how to deal with it. The man had been in charge of the country, and now, he wasn't anymore. That didn't mean Mery didn't need him, but he should be doing more than what he was doing if Mery was to be king. He might need the prime minister's help, but the man shouldn't be doing Mery's job.

Mery sighed. This was yet another problem he was supposed to solve and didn't know how to. Hopefully, Sed would be able to advise him since he'd met hundreds of kings. If he couldn't, well, Mery would have to find another way. He wasn't sure there was one, but he supposed he would find out soon enough.

He relaxed on the bench, intent on spending some time alone now that Sed was gone. He had all of five minutes of peace before a woman called out, "Your majesty?"

Mery almost groaned. He wanted to ignore her, but he thought he recognized Tayet's voice. It wouldn't be good to ignore a god, no matter how minor.

Mery got to his feet and looked around. Sure enough, the goddess was at his bedroom door, looking out. Mery sighed and moved toward her. "Good morning," he said.

She smiled, still as gentle as she'd been yesterday. "I wanted to know what you thought of the clothes I left you. I need to get you many more, but I'd like to know which one you prefer first. There's also the coronation ceremony and party to think about."

This was part of Mery's job as the king, too. No matter how little he cared about the clothes he wore, he had to look royal. Who better than Tayet to make sure he did?

CHAPTER THREE

"I just don't understand why you brought him here," Sed's mother complained.

Sed and Jimmy looked at each other. Jimmy had tried to reassure Sed that he didn't mind that his mother acted like he wasn't even in the room most of the time, but Sed was pissed. He realized his mother wasn't used to dealing with humans, but that didn't mean she had to be rude. Jimmy had been nice to her since they'd arrived yesterday, yet she still looked at him like he was dirt on the bottom of her shoes — when she looked at him at all. Right now, it was as if Jimmy wasn't even sitting at the breakfast table with them.

Sed didn't want to make his mother angry, not when he might need her to help Mery, but he also wasn't going to allow her to treat Jimmy the way she was. "I brought him here because he's my best friend," he said through gritted teeth.

"I don't understand that, either," she said. She snagged a strawberry from a bowl at the center of the table. "You used to be so close to your cousin. He could be your best friend."

"Which cousin are you talking about?"

"Qebui, of course."

"We were close, but we're not anymore. And I'm not going to change my best friend. I've lived with Jimmy for years, and he's not going anywhere. I'm sorry if you don't like it, but please, can you stop being rude to him?"

Sed's mother's eyes blazed. If there was one thing she didn't like, it was being called rude. She knew she was, though, which was why she didn't protest. Instead, she looked at Jimmy. Her expression told Sed she was afraid he would do something he shouldn't, but at least she was finally looking at him as if he were a person. "I apologize if I made you feel like you weren't welcome," she said.

Jimmy cleared his throat. "It's fine. I realize you didn't expect my presence, and I'm grateful I was allowed to stay."

Sed wanted to snort, but he knew better. This wasn't the celestial palace, so his mother didn't have a say on who was allowed to stay here. Mery was the only one who did, and while Sed hadn't seen him since yesterday when they'd talked in the garden, he was pretty sure the man wouldn't mind Jimmy's presence.

Sed's mother turned her attention back to him. "All right. I have a list of things you need to do and people you'll have to talk to. And of course, parties I expect you to attend. People are happy to know you're back, and they're eager to see you."

Sed stared at his mother. She was doing what he'd expected her to do—steamrolling him and deciding what he was supposed to do and not do. She also seemed to have assumed he was here to stay, which couldn't be further from the truth. "I won't have time to go to parties and talk to people," he said slowly. He didn't want to anger her, but he knew he would anyway since he wasn't doing what she wanted.

"Of course you do. I realize you have to work with the new king, but surely it won't last long. Once he goes through the coronation ceremony, your job will be done, and you'll be able to focus on your family. You won't have to stay here after that, and your rooms are still the way you left them." She paused and peeked at Jimmy. "Although your best friend might be a problem. There's never been a human in the celestial palace. I doubt he'll be allowed to stay with us."

Sed sighed. "Mother, I understand you're happy to see me after all those years, but don't do this."

She looked at him like she didn't understand what he was

saying, and maybe she didn't. Before leaving, he'd allowed her to tell him what to do with his life. It had been easier than going against her will. He wasn't willing to do that anymore, and she had to understand that.

"Don't do what?" she asked.

"Don't make plans. As soon as it's fine for me to go home, I'll go. I'm not staying here, and I'm not visiting the celestial palace."

"Why not? It's your home."

"It was once, but it hasn't been in years. When I say I'm going home, I mean to the United States."

She opened her mouth, no doubt to argue and tell him how much she missed him and that he shouldn't mingle with humans, but he was done talking about this. He'd told her his intention and how he felt, and no amount of repeating himself would convince her he wasn't staying. She'd only learn when she saw him leave, but in the meantime, he had things to do and to focus on. "Tell me about the new king," he interrupted.

She huffed, but thankfully, she went along with it. "What do you want to know? I haven't even met him."

"Who did? And who decided we needed a king again?"

"I'm not sure. I heard about it from Min, but it no doubt came from higher up. Your cousin thinks it was an order from Ra, and I agree. The old man wouldn't allow something like this to happen if he didn't agree with it."

"And Mery was chosen because he descends from the pharaohs."

"The old ones, yes, not the Greek ones."

Sed hadn't even considered them. Even though the Greek pharaohs had revered the old gods, they'd been Greek. Most of the gods in his family didn't view them as Egyptians. "What can you tell me about the people around him?"

"How am I supposed to know? I told you I've never met him."

"But something is going on, and I'm sure you're aware of that. They're going to manipulate him, and it would make sense for a god to be behind that."

Sed's mother looked offended. "Why should we have anything to do with this?"

"Because it's what we've always done. Gods meddle in humans' lives. I don't see why this situation should be any different. Ra might have given the order to choose a new king, but everyone is going to try to take advantage of that, and of Mery."

"Well, I wouldn't, and I don't know what you're talking about." She got to her feet. "And I expect you to attend at least a few parties. We're your family, even though you haven't treated us like it for a long time."

Then she was gone in a flurry of long gowns and perfume. Sed sighed and leaned back in his chair. It was only breakfast, but he already had a headache.

"So that's your mom," Jimmy said. Thankfully, he sounded amused rather than offended.

"It is. I'm sorry for the way she's been treating you."

Jimmy shrugged. "Honestly, I didn't expect anything different from her or anyone else. They're gods. I realize you're an oddity."

Sed was, and he didn't like it. Jimmy might be human, but that didn't mean he didn't deserve to be treated with respect.

"Besides, not being important to her or the other gods comes in handy sometimes," Jimmy continued.

Sed was surprised. "What do you mean?"

"Yesterday, while you were busy with the king, I went around the palace. I just wanted to explore, but I found more than I expected."

Sed straightened. "What?"

"The servants were more than happy to talk to me about which gods have been hanging around the palace. Your cousin has been around a lot, while your mother just arrived for the first time yesterday, the same as we did. They mentioned a goddess named Tayet, too."

"She's the one who takes care of the king's clothing. She's probably planning what he'll wear for the coronation ceremony and the party after it."

Jimmy nodded. "I didn't know that. They also mentioned a guy named Anhur? He's been visiting the prime minister."

Sed grabbed a strawberry and bit half of it off. Tayet's presence was normal, but Anhur? He was a minor god of war and patron of the army. It might make sense for him to visit the prime minister if it had to do with the military, but Sed didn't like this.

Something big was at play here, and Sed was only now starting to understand. If he wanted to keep his promise to Mery, he would have to work hard to find out what was happening and why.

Mery almost groaned when someone found him in the garden today, too, but he stopped when he realized it was a man he'd never seen. He stood out in the palace with his pale skin and even more so with the black dog following him. He wouldn't be here if he weren't allowed, so Mery wasn't too worried, but he still stared as the man came closer.

The man smiled. "I'm Jimmy."

Mery had no idea who that was. "I'm Mery."

Jimmy's eyes widened. "You're the king, right? Sed mentioned you."

So he was a friend of Sed? His paleness made more sense now. "You arrived here with Sed?"

Jimmy nodded and gestured at the stone bench on which Mery was sitting. "Do you mind? I don't want to bother you, so don't feel obligated, but I'd rather sit down if we're going to talk."

"Feel free." Talking with someone who wasn't a god or a servant would be a nice change. Hopefully, Jimmy would treat Mery like a normal person, like people had treated Mery before.

Jimmy sat next to Mery. The dog curled at their feet, and Mery couldn't help but reach for it. He stopped before touching it, looking at Jimmy, who nodded.

"He's a nice dog. He's Sed's, which is why he's here."

"What's his name?"

Jimmy's smile widened. "Loki. And yes, I know he's a god from another pantheon. That's why I thought it would be fun."

Mery couldn't help but smile back as he stroked Loki's head. "I think it is. I wasn't aware that Sed had arrived with a friend."

"I don't think a lot of people are happy to see me here, to be honest. I'm almost tempted to ask him to take me back to Pittsburgh. I would if I still had my job, but I was fired recently, so I don't have anything to go back to."

There was pain in Jimmy's voice, but Mery wasn't sure how to help. He wasn't sure he could, even though he was the king. "I'm sorry about that. I hope everyone is treating you okay."

"A few gods have been rude, and one guy looked like he wanted to have me kicked out, but I guess he knew better."

"Can you tell me about your life in the United States?" Mery wanted to talk about anything that would distract him from his own life here at the palace. It would only be for a few moments, but it would be better than nothing.

Thankfully, Jimmy smiled and nodded. He started talking, and Mery was able to lose himself in the details of a life he would never live. It didn't last nearly long enough for him, but when a man appeared in front of them, making both of them jump, he got to his feet. The only people who could appear the way this man had were gods, which meant he was one.

Mery bowed at the man, but Jimmy stayed seated.

"Sed isn't here," he told the god.

"I'm aware, since I can't see him."

"Why are you here, then?" Jimmy asked.

The god stared at Jimmy, and Mery held his breath. It would be nothing for him to hurt Jimmy for the way he was talking to him. Mery breathed easier when the god shook his head. "I was bored."

"And you decided to come to bother us?" Jimmy responded.

Mery sucked in a breath. "I apologize," he said.

The god shrugged. "You don't have to. I'm getting used to him." He stared at Mery. "I'm Qebui."

Mery nodded. "God of the North winds. It's a pleasure to meet you."

Qebui looked delighted. "Finally, someone who recognizes me. You're the new king."

"I am, although I haven't gone through the coronation ceremony yet." Mery cautiously sat again.

To Mery's surprise, Qebui settled between him and Jimmy. They both had to slide sideways to make enough space for him, and while Jimmy looked annoyed, Mery didn't mind. Before coming to the palace, he'd never talked to a god. He'd never even seen one, and he was still surprised every time he met one. Qebui was acting as if he were one of them—a human—which didn't make much sense.

"What were the two of you talking about?" Qebui asked. He was staring at Jimmy as he talked, so Mery was pretty sure he wasn't talking to him.

"Really, what do you want?" Jimmy asked.

"I realize I was rude when I first met you. I'm trying to

apologize and show you I'm a good person."

"You're ignoring Mery."

Mery wanted to tell Jimmy he didn't mind, but Qebui turned toward him and tilted his head forward. "I apologize for that, too. Please, act as if I were a mere human. I realize it might be hard, but I truly want to get to know the two of you."

"Because I'm your messenger?" Mery asked.

Qebui hesitated. "In part, but also because I'm curious." He looked at Jimmy again. "I never realized how nice humans could be. I don't often leave the celestial palace, so I never got the chance to really talk to humans. Knowing that Sed has been living with Jimmy for years and that they're friends made me want to know more."

Mery was more than happy to let Jimmy take the lead. He didn't think Qebui was a bad person, but he was still a god, which meant Mery was wary. He didn't know if there was anyone he could trust except for his family, but unfortunately, he hadn't been able to talk to them in a while.

Every time he tried to get into their wing in the palace, the guards stopped him. He'd mentioned it to Ibuki, but the PA always brushed him off, saying it was a mistake before dragging Mery back to his office to work. That meant Mery hadn't been able to see his family in a few weeks, and he missed them. He also missed being able to trust someone entirely, and he wanted that back.

Thinking about Ibuki seemed to make him appear. He stepped out of Mery's private rooms, which made Mery bristle. He didn't want anyone to be there except for him and the people he wanted there.

"There you are," he said, walking into the garden. "I've been looking for you everywhere. You should be in your office."

Mery got to his feet, but before he could say anything, Qebui intervened. "Is that how you talk to your king?" he asked, his eyes blazing — literally.

Ibuki froze. He probably hadn't realized who Qebui he was until now. He bowed, not looking up but instead keeping his focus on his feet. "I apologize."

"As you should. Meryatum is your king, and you should treat him like it."

"And I already told you I don't want you or anyone else in my private rooms," Mery added. He might not have had the courage to say that to Ibuki's face if Qebui hadn't been here, but having a god supporting him helped.

"I apologize again, your majesty. I shouldn't have come in, but I was looking for you."

"Whatever you need, it can wait."

"I'm afraid it can't. I'm putting together the menu for the coronation ceremony party, and I—"

"Do whatever you want with the party. I don't care." Mery wasn't planning on partying anyway.

He was doing what he had to do, but that didn't mean he liked it. He'd never been big on parties, but at least the ones he'd attended in the past included family. He wouldn't know most of the people who would be there after his coronation ceremony. He wasn't looking forward to the ceremony or the party.

"But, your majesty—"

"You heard him," Qebui snapped. "Let him be. Whatever you need to ask, I'm sure you can find someone else to make that decision. The king has other things to focus on."

Mery couldn't see Ibuki's expression, but he could easily read the man's straight spine and tight fists. He was angry, but he wouldn't say anything about it, not in front of a god.

Mery suspected Ibuki wouldn't have been nearly as respectful if Qebui hadn't been here. It was a problem, but not something Mery wanted to face right now. His problems weren't going anywhere anyway. He would have to

43

discipline Ibuki and possibly find another personal assistant, but not right now.

Now, he wanted to act as if he still was a normal man talking with his friends and not think about the gods, the kingship, or anything else.

Sed had been looking for Qebui, so he was relieved to find him in the garden. He and Jimmy were walking along a path, Loki running around them, and Sed took a moment to look at them. Qebui appeared like he was behaving nicely enough, so Sed wouldn't say anything, but he was still worried about his best friend. It was easy to become infatuated with a god, but it never ended well, especially for a human.

But Jimmy was an adult, and he knew what he was doing, or at least, Sed hoped so. Sed would make sure to talk to him if he thought things were going the wrong way, but he couldn't force Jimmy to do or not do something, and he didn't want to try. He never wanted to play god with Jimmy especially, but he would be there for him as a friend.

Jimmy saw him first and waved at him. "What have you been up to? Did your mother find you again?"

Sed shook his head. "I haven't seen her since breakfast." And he was more than happy to keep things that way. He loved his mother, but the relationship was complicated, and it was one problem he didn't need right now.

"I don't understand why you're so annoyed with her," Qebui said.

Sed arched a brow. "You know my mother. How can you not understand?"

Qebui shrugged. "I suppose I'm more used to her. She and I have been closer since you left."

That should make Sed feel guilty, and it did, but he pushed it away. He loved his mother, and that would never change, but she was a lot to deal with, and he didn't have time for it. "I was looking for you," he told Qebui.

Qebui frowned. "What did I do this time?"

"Nothing as far as I know, although if you can think of something, please tell me."

"I'm not an idiot."

"I'm not sure I agree. But I just wanted to talk to you about some of our cousins." Sed wasn't sure he was related to An-hur, but in a way, all gods were cousins. He had no idea who Anhur's parents were, and he didn't care, either.

"You're already ditching me for someone more interesting?"

There was a hint of pain in Qebui's voice, and it made Sed wonder. He'd missed his cousin, and he knew Qebui had missed him, but they hadn't been close in a long time. He hadn't expected Qebui to care about the distance between them, but maybe he'd been wrong. Maybe once he went back home, he should keep Qebui in mind and try to be closer to him.

That was, if Qebui stopped being so annoying.

"I'm not ditching you for anyone. You might be annoying, but you're my cousin."

"It didn't mean much to you when you left."

Sed sighed. He and Qebui were going to have to talk about this eventually, but he wasn't ready. "It was a mistake. I ran because I wanted to be away from all the drama and how overwhelming my mother was, and I didn't think of you. I should have, and I'm sorry. Right now, though, I have to focus on the king, because I think something is happening. I need your help, Qebui."

Qebui's expression hardened. Sed expected him to be angry that he was reaching out to him only because he needed him, but instead, he said, "Tell me."

"You and I both know something is wrong. I don't know

why Ra suddenly decided he wanted to put a king on the throne, but I don't think that matters. What does matter is what the other gods are doing. Jimmy told me Anhur has been around, talking to the prime minister, and I know the prime minister isn't allowing Mery to do his job."

"And you think Anhur has something to do with it?"

"Isn't it strange that another minor god has been hanging around the palace?"

"I'm a minor god, and I've been hanging around the palace," Qebui said. "It's strange, but you know how things are in the celestial palace. Some of us get bored, and we don't get to move to the United States."

"You could if you wanted to, but can we please focus on this?"

"We are. I don't think there's anything strange with minor gods being around. We're all curious about the new king and what his presence will mean for us. That's why *I'm* here."

He looked at Jimmy as he spoke, and Sed was sure there was more to it. Now wasn't the moment to talk to Qebui about Jimmy, no matter how much he wanted to. He'd promised Mery he would take care of him and help him as much as he could, and he intended to do just that. He hoped Qebui would be there with him, but maybe he shouldn't have counted his cousin in before talking to him.

"Anhur is the god of war."

Qebui snorted. "A *minor* god of war. I doubt he's going to do anything."

"Then it shouldn't be a problem for you to help me."

Qebui looked wary. "What do you need me to do?"

"Go to the celestial palace and poke around, please. I want to find out why Anhur is visiting the palace."

"Come on, Sed. You haven't been away from us long enough to forget everything about us. We visit the human world because we're *bored*. That's probably why Anhur is at the palace."

"Maybe that's the case, but I want to be sure."

"What do you think is going to happen?"

"I don't know what he's up to, but I'm worried someone might try to hurt Mery, and soon. He's the king, but he's never done anything like this. He's only been here for a few weeks longer than I have, and he's lost. It would be too easy for a god to manipulate him, and I think that's what people are trying to do." And not just the gods. Sed didn't like Mery's assistant, and while he hadn't spoken to the prime minister yet, he was pretty sure the man was involved in this, too. "I'm the protector of kingship and the king, so this is my job. I can do it alone if you don't want to help, but it would be easier if you agreed to this. Besides, I *want* to work with you."

Qebui stared at Sed for long enough that Sed thought he would say no. He would be sorry, but he hadn't been lying when he'd said he would do this on his own. His job was to protect Mery and help him, and it didn't matter to him that he had to go against other gods to do it. It was an everyday occurrence in the celestial palace, which was one reason he'd left.

"Fine. I'll poke around and see what people are saying," Qebui finally said.

Sed could have kissed him. "Thank you. I know you don't believe me, but I'm grateful."

"I do believe you. I just wish you'd want to spend time with me for something other than the king."

And there was the guilt again. "We can spend as much time together as you want once I'm sure Mery is safe."

"We'll see." Qebui turned to Jimmy. "I need to go. I'll see you soon?"

Jimmy seemed amused. "You know where to find me. I'm not going anywhere."

Qebui nodded. Then he was gone, leaving Jimmy and Sed

alone. Loki had spread out in a patch of shade as they talked, and he looked like he was sleeping. Sed moved closer to Jimmy. "You need to be careful."

Jimmy didn't look surprised. "I know you think I don't know what I'm doing, and maybe you're right. He's not going to hurt me, though."

"Not physically, no." But mentally, emotionally? Qebui just might.

A lot of gods viewed humans as tools for their amusement. They didn't care how many people they hurt or how. As long as they had their fun, they didn't stop for anything. Qebui wasn't like that exactly, but he often didn't understand how much he could hurt humans.

But if he hurt Jimmy, he would have to deal with Sed.

Mery wished he could go back outside with Jimmy and Qebui, but instead, he was behind his desk, scowling at a stack of documents in front of him. "What's all this?"

Ibuki grinned. It looked slightly menacing, which didn't bode well for Mery. "Everything you need to know about what I organized for the coronation ceremony and the party after it. You need to go over it and approve it."

"I told you I didn't care about those things. Do whatever you want."

"I can't. I might be a personal assistant, but you're the king. It's your job to do this."

"My job should be governing the country, not reading menus for a party I don't even want to attend."

Ibuki scowled and crossed his arms over his chest. "Your job is to do what a king should do, which includes this. I realize it's boring, but you can't just ignore the boring parts of the job. You've been asking to be allowed to do more, and now that you are, you complain again. I didn't think I would ever say this, but you sound ungrateful, and you should focus on your job as king instead of going around the gardens making friends with weird people. This is an honor, and you agreed to it."

Mery stared at Ibuki in shock. His PA had never dared talk to him that way. No one had, not since he'd arrived at the palace. Mery wasn't sure how to react. He was offended, but he also couldn't help but wonder if Ibuki was right.

Mery *had* been complaining about the job. The only thing he'd been able to focus on was how much freedom agreeing to be king had taken away from him. That didn't mean he didn't want to do what was expected of him, but he really didn't think that focusing on parties was that important. He should be working with the prime minister and learning how to do his job, not talking wine.

"If you didn't want to do this, you shouldn't have accepted the job," Ibuki continued. "We could have found someone better suited."

Mery opened his mouth to answer, but before he could, a man said, "That's bullshit, and you shouldn't talk to your king that way."

For the second time in a handful of hours, Mery had been saved by a god. Sed stepped in through the open door that led to the gardens. He looked angrier than Mery had ever seen him, although since he didn't really know him, it didn't mean much. Thankfully, he wasn't glaring at Mery but rather at Ibuki.

Mery's assistant looked like he was about to self-combust. "Sir, I apologize—"

"I'm not who you should apologize to. You showed disrespect to the king, and if I were him, I would fire you and find myself another personal assistant."

"That's not possible. The prime minister assigned me to this job personally."

Sed arched a brow. "And the prime minister has more power than the king?"

Ibuki spluttered, but thankfully, he didn't dig his grave any deeper. He looked from Sed to Mery. Then he stood up straighter. "I apologize, your highness. I realize this is a boring part of the job, and of course, as long as you don't care, I can take care of it. There are some documents you do have to go over in that pile, though. Amongst it is a list of women."

Mery blinked. "A list of women?"

"That you should consider for marriage. We can have the ceremony in a few months, after you go through the coronation ceremony."

"We never talked about marriage," Mery said, his stomach feeling like he had turned to stone.

"The prime minister put this list together, and he's right. You ought to have an heir, and the sooner you can produce one, the better it will be for the country."

That made Mery feel like a prized bull, and once again, he was thankful to Sed for intervening.

"The king doesn't have to do anything he doesn't want, and that includes marrying a woman he's never met. Leave us. I'm sure you have work to do," he told Ibuki.

Ibuki huffed and grabbed part of the pile of documents that were on Mery's desk. He left without looking back, leaving the door open. Mery should have been angry, but he was too tired for that.

"You need to stand up for yourself," Sed said as he moved closer to the desk.

Mery rubbed his forehead. "I know. I'm just not sure when I can and can't do it."

"Do it any time you think they're taking advantage of you." He grabbed a piece of paper from the pile of documents.

Mery wondered what he was looking at. He looked even angrier than before. "I'm pretty sure they're taking advantage of me every second of every day."

Sed slowly nodded. "You're probably right. I'm not surprised to see the prime minister's niece on this list."

"I have no idea what you're talking about."

Sed walked to the door and closed it. Once he was done, he came back to the desk and sat on the other side of it, facing Mery. He put down the piece of paper he'd been reading, and leaning closer, Mery could see it was a list of names.

Names of the women he was supposed to consider for marriage.

Sed tapped his index finger on one of the names. "Aneksi. I've been looking into the prime minister and your personal assistant. So far, I haven't found much, but I know this woman is his niece. He wants you to marry into his family."

Mery wasn't surprised. "He wants to be linked to the king."

"And it would be great for him if his niece gave the king an heir. It would put him one step closer to the throne if something happened to you."

That didn't surprise Mery, either. He'd expected someone to try to get rid of him eventually. He just hadn't thought it would happen so soon. "You think he wants to kill me?"

"Not yet, and I can't be a hundred percent sure. I don't want to talk badly about someone when I don't know them, but it's something to consider, especially since I know a minor god has been visiting him. But he was in power until you were chosen as king. He's been avoiding teaching you how to do your job, and he's been doing it in your place. It's clear to me he doesn't want to give it up, and if you died, it would make it easier for him. It would be even easier if you died after getting married and having a son. If the child was young enough, he wouldn't be able to take your place on the throne, and either his mother or the prime minister would do it for him."

Mery groaned. "I don't want to get married."

"You might not have a choice."

"If I have to, I want to marry someone I love."

When Mery looked up, Sed was smiling at him. It was a sad smile, unfortunately. "You should be able to. Some of the pharaohs that came before you were strong enough to stand up against everyone, and they had marriages of love. Others were not, followed tradition, and allowed someone else to pick their spouse for them. You can choose what kind of king you want to be. You're young, still learning how to deal with this, and no one will be surprised if you stand up for yourself. You can't allow them to beat you down, not if you want to make the most of what you have."

"I might be king, but I don't have any real power."

"You could. I can help you with that, and we can work toward you taking your rightful place on the throne. That means dealing with things that will be unpleasant to deal with, though. Are you ready to do that?"

Mery wasn't, but what choice did he have? He couldn't allow Ibuki and the prime minister to reign in his place. He'd agreed to be king, and he had to act like one, no matter how awkward or hard it was. He had to stop allowing everyone to walk all over him and finally start to make decisions the way a king would.

Nothing had ever sounded harder.

CHAPTER FOUR

Mery stared at himself in the mirror. His heart was racing, and he couldn't recognize the man staring back at him.

He'd always dressed simply. He hadn't needed to dress any other way, not when he'd been a farmer. He was used to a modest life, and that included modest clothing. What he was wearing right now was anything but.

It was the first time he looked at himself and saw a king.

The parties and festivities for his coronation had already started all over the city, probably all over the country. Mery was pretty sure most people didn't understand much of what was happening, but the gods had spoken, so everyone went along with it—including him.

He felt like something would go wrong, but it was only a vague inkling. He and Sed had been working together since Sed had arrived a few weeks ago, and Mery would never be more ready than he already was.

They'd gone over the various ceremonies he'd have to go through several times, often enough that he could recite them from memory. The problem was that knowing what was supposed to happen didn't make it easier to go through it. If Mery still had one chance to get out of this, it would vanish as soon as he went through with the ceremonies. By the end of the day, he would be king, and there would be no going back.

Mery hadn't had to attend his predecessor's funeral, since he didn't have one. He was relieved, since that meant they got to skip right to the next stage of the ceremony, and he wouldn't have to deal with a dead body.

Someone knocked on the door, and he was happy to step away from the mirror. The door opened when he called out, and one of the guards stepped in. "Your highness. The god Qebui and his friend want to talk to you."

"Let them in and close the door behind them."

The guard nodded and obeyed. Once Qebui and Jimmy were in Mery's private rooms, the door closed behind them. He breathed easier, but not as easily as he wished. He wanted to tear off the clothes he was wearing and go back to being only Mery.

"How are you doing?" Jimmy asked gently.

"I have no idea."

Jimmy's expression turned to pity, and while Mery wasn't happy to see it, he pitied himself, so why shouldn't Jimmy pity him? "Everything will be fine. Sed is really proud of how easily you learned everything you need to know. Besides, he'll be there with you."

That was the only reason Mery wasn't entirely freaking out. He wasn't doing this alone. Sed would be there like he'd been there for him since he'd arrived. Mery didn't know what he would do without the god, and he didn't want to start thinking about that. He had more than enough reasons to freak out right now without adding another one to the pile.

"You look good," Qebui said.

Mery looked down at himself. He wasn't as luxuriously dressed as he'd expected. Instead, his chest and feet were bare, his hair loose—it had grown since he'd arrived at the palace and he needed a haircut, but Sed had convinced him to wait until after the ceremony—and he was wearing a traditional white skirt. He had jewelry on, of course, but it wasn't ostentatious. It was just enough to let everyone know who he was. "Thank you," he said.

"You know you don't have to go through with it if you don't want to," Jimmy said.

Mery took a deep breath. "I understand. I *do* have to go through with it, though. I don't have a choice, not anymore." He hadn't had a choice since he'd agreed to come to the palace and do this. "I'll be fine. I'm just nervous."

"As anyone would be in your place," Qebui said. "I remember some of the old coronation ceremonies. You'll be fine. Just follow Sed's cues and do what he told you to do. Everything will be okay."

Mery hoped he was right.

There was another knock on the door, and this time, it was a servant who came to fetch him to start the ceremony. After one last glance at Jimmy and Qebui, Mery followed the man down the hallway and out of the palace.

Sed met him at the temple, and like Mery, he was wearing a white skirt and his hair was loose. He looked like a normal human being instead of a god, and Mery couldn't look away. Sed's skin appeared smooth in the afternoon light, and he smiled when he saw Mery. Mery wanted to go to him, but he wasn't allowed. He had to focus on what was about to happen, no matter how panicky it made him feel and how much he wanted to run away.

He nodded at Sed, and Sed nodded at him. Together, they turned toward the entrance of the temple.

Mery could smell the heady scent of incense coming from inside, mingled with chanting voices. The inside of the temple was dark, as it was supposed to be. Mery wished he'd been able to see a video of what was about to happen, but he had only Sed's words to rely on. When he walked through the door, he would still be only Mery. When he left, he would be Meryatum, the pharaoh. He would have paid tribute to the gods of Upper and Lower Egypt while wearing the crowns of both those territories, and they would become one before he stepped out, signaling that he ruled over the entire country with the gods' approval.

Talk about expectations.

There was no turning back, and as Mery took one step, then another, he tried to stand up straighter. Thanks to Sed, he knew what he was doing. This was going to change his life, and it might not be for the better, but he wasn't going back on his word.

He was the pharaoh. He couldn't.

Sed was proud of Mery. He'd watched dozens of coronation ceremonies, and Mery had behaved better than half the other pharaohs. He'd been calm and collected, and he'd remembered everything Sed had taught him. Now the ceremony was over, and the party could begin.

It already had all over the city. It was loud and boisterous, but Mery looked anything but. Even now at the palace party, he was sitting on his throne looking down at the people who had come to celebrate with him, but he wasn't mingling.

Sed understood why. Mery had never wanted this, and he was doing it for his family, whom Sed had met. Mery's mother was hovering close to the throne, talking to a man in a dark blue suit. She looked just like Mery, and while she was smiling, she kept looking at her son with a small frown on her face.

"Your presence here means you approve of the new king," Sed's mother said from behind him.

He almost groaned. He didn't have the energy to face her, not after the ceremony. She'd been there, too, although Sed hadn't seen her. He'd been more focused on Mery than on anything or anyone else.

He turned to face her. "I do approve of the new king," he told her.

She stared at him for a moment before nodding. "I agree with you. He seems like a good man."

"He is. Unfortunately, his problems have only just begun."

"Isn't that always the case when it comes to kings?" She took a sip of the drink she was holding. "When will you be leaving, then?"

Sed stared at her for a moment before understanding what she was saying. "I'm not going anywhere."

She looked surprised. "I thought you were only here because you had to be, not because you wanted to. Your job is done. The king is on the throne, and he doesn't need you anymore. You're free to go back to your life."

It was a far cry from the way she'd behaved when Sed had first come back. He'd finally managed to convince her he wasn't staying just in time for him to decide he'd stick around for a bit longer. He still didn't trust Ibuki and the prime minister, and he wasn't about to leave Mery unprotected. He would never forgive himself if something happened to him and he wasn't here to prevent it.

But it was more than that. He wanted to protect Mery, but he also wanted to spend more time with him. He realized how dangerous that was. It would be far too easy for him to fall in love with the king, and maybe he was already partly there. Spending so much time with Mery, teaching him how to go through the ceremony, had brought them closer than Sed had ever been to a human except for Jimmy. He didn't want to leave because he didn't want to be away from Mery.

That was the reason he *should* go away, but he couldn't find it in himself to do it. He knew he could leave Mery's protection in Qebui's hands. His cousin might be snobbish and volatile, but he was a good person, and Sed trusted him.

But for once, he wanted to do what every other god did. So many of them had fallen in love with humans and had been with them. Sed always stayed away from that kind of relationship, not knowing if he would be strong enough to watch the person he loved age and die. He also hadn't wanted to bring the complications of being a god into those people's lives.

But Mery was different. The gods were already running amok in his life, and it wasn't going to change anytime soon. He was the king, and his main job was to be a messenger for the gods. He would have contact with them for the rest of his life, so Sed didn't have to stay away from him if he didn't want to.

And he didn't.

He cleared his throat. He had to give his mother an answer, and while she would be delighted to learn he was staying, it also meant she would be all over him. "I still feel Mery needs help."

"He has the prime minister and an army of servants for that."

"He does. Something is going on, though, and I want to be here for him if he needs me."

Sed's mother kept staring. "You like him."

"Why is that so surprising? You'd like him, too, if you got to know him."

"That's not what I was talking about. You like him as more than a friend."

Sed shook his head. He didn't want to expose his feelings to anyone, least of all his mother. "I like him because he's a good person and will be a good king if he's given the opportunity. Now, if you'll excuse me, I see Jimmy."

Sed kissed his mother's cheek and walked away. He *had* seen Jimmy, who looked dashing in traditional ancient Egyptian clothes. The clothes were odd on him since his skin was so pale, and he stood out more than anyone but Mery, but he was gorgeous, and Sed wasn't the only one who'd noticed. Qebui had been staring at Jimmy as if he were the main course, and while it made Sed uneasy, he had no say in what was happening between Qebui and Jimmy—if anything was happening at all. It was none of his business, and Jimmy knew he could come to him if he needed help or advice. That was all Sed could do and all he was *willing* to do.

This was why he didn't want to visit his family. Even when they didn't intend to, they managed to create drama, and he had no doubt that was what would happen if Qebui started dating Jimmy. Some of the gods wouldn't be happy, and even though most wouldn't care since they'd done the same thing at one time, the unhappy ones were always the more vocal. They would make sure Qebui knew what they thought about him needing a human, and they might even try to stop him from doing it. It would be a mess, and it was a mess Sed didn't want anything to do with.

He walked around the room, staying close to the walls. His presence was enough to tell everyone he approved of the king, but he didn't want most people to notice him if at all possible. He was looking for clues, and he thought he found one when he noticed Ibuki talking with a tall woman in a corner.

She was beautiful. She was wearing a long red dress, and her arms, neck, and ears dripped with jewels. Her long black hair was artistically pulled up, and her makeup was perfect. Ibuki didn't seem interested in her body, though. They were talking, their heads close, and they kept peeking at Mery, who looked as bored as he had ten minutes ago.

Sed wanted to know who the woman was, but he didn't know who to ask. He looked around, hoping Qebui could tell him, and his eyes widened when he saw Nu sipping on a drink nearby.

They were his great-great-great-grandparent—or something like that. Nu was the god from whom the first gods had been born, and they didn't usually leave the celestial palace. Sed had only seen them a few times thousands of years ago, so their presence here was strange, but it also meant a lot.

Luckily, Sed and Nu had always gotten along, and he made his way toward them.

"I didn't expect you to be here," he told them when he reached them.

They smiled at him. "The first king in thousands of years. I couldn't miss it."

They were wearing a simple white dress that stopped above their knee. They looked no older than fifty, but Sed knew the truth. They were the oldest god anyone could remember.

"What do you think, then?" he asked.

"I think that your presence here says a lot."

"Meryatum will be a great king."

"If he's allowed to be." Nu's gaze was shrewd. "Why were you staring at the king's personal assistant?"

"You always see everything, don't you?"

Nu's smile widened. "It's something I'm known for. So?"

Sed leaned closer. "I think the prime minister and the king's personal assistant are plotting with a few minor gods. They want the power, and they can't have it until Mery is taken care of."

"Tell me."

It was an order, and Sed obeyed. He told Nu everything he knew, even though it wasn't a lot. So far, he only had suspicions, and they weren't enough to confront the people involved. Nu nodded as Sed spoke, and once he was done, he stared at them.

"That woman talking to the personal assistant. She's the prime minister's niece."

Sed should have realized that. She'd been on the list of women Mery was supposed to consider for marriage, and Sed had suspected she had something to do with this. He'd hoped she was innocent, but he knew better.

"How do you know all of this?" he asked. "You barely

leave your rooms in the celestial palace, yet you seem to know everything there is to know about everyone here."

"I have my ways. And I agree with you that something is happening. What will you do about it?"

Sed wasn't sure yet, but of one thing, he was.

He would keep Mery safe, whatever that entailed.

Mery was bored. He'd never enjoyed parties, not even family parties, and this was even worse. There were a lot of people, and he only knew a few of them. He was pretty sure that only a few of them cared about him, too.

He wanted to climb off the throne and find his mother and his siblings. He wanted to spend time with them and ignore everyone else. He'd tried to do just that, but Ibuki had been there, stopping him and getting him back on the throne, murmuring things Mery hadn't listened to because he didn't care. He didn't care about any of this.

He was exhausted and wanted to go to bed, but instead, he was stuck on the throne.

He supposed things could be worse. From where he was, he could keep an eye on Sed, who'd been walking around the room and talking to a few people. Mery had recognized Sed's his mother, but not the older woman Sed was talking to now. He didn't think who the woman was mattered. What mattered was that he had feelings for Sed, feelings he shouldn't be having.

Because Sed wasn't just a man. He was a god, and now that his job here was done, he would leave. He'd talked about his life in the United States often enough that Mery was sure of that. Sed wouldn't give it up for anything, and he shouldn't have to. He *didn't* have to, not when he only viewed Mery as a friend. The fact that Mery didn't was a problem only he had to deal with, and he would keep it to himself.

"Your highness," Ibuki said as he came closer.

A woman was walking next to him, and while Mery was pretty sure he'd seen her somewhere, he didn't remember where or even why she mattered. She had to if she was here, but he didn't like the way she was looking at him. It was almost as if she were planning on eating him, which he wouldn't put past anyone in the room.

"This is Aneksi, the prime minister's niece. He thought it would be nice for me to introduce her to you."

Mery stared. He'd looked at the list of women Ibuki had put together only once before stuffing it into a drawer and promising himself he would never look at it again, and Aneksi's name was on it. He didn't care who was on it—he wasn't marrying any of them. He couldn't say that to her face, though, so instead, he smiled. "I hope you're enjoying yourself."

She bowed. "I am, your majesty. Everyone in the country is happy to have you as our guide."

That was bullshit, and Mery almost snorted. He noticed Ibuki gently pushing Aneksi closer to the throne, and he shot to his feet, startling both of them.

Mery cleared his throat. "I apologize. I need to go."

"Where?" Ibuki asked.

Once again, he was asking too many questions, and they were questions he wasn't entitled to get an answer to. "I don't think it's any of your business."

"I'm your personal assistant, which makes it my business. I'm here to help you, whatever you need."

Mery arched a brow. "Does that include helping me in the bathroom?"

Ibuki's cheeks turned a dark red. "I apologize, your highness."

He was flustered, and Mery took advantage of it. He climbed down the steps that led to the throne, walked around

Ibuki and Aneksi, and tried to lose himself in the crowd.

It wasn't easy. Now that he was away from the throne, a lot of people wanted to talk to him. He smiled at them and talked to a few, but he had a goal, and he wasn't giving up.

He'd had enough of this.

He paused for a moment when he saw his mother, but he didn't want to interrupt her chat with a tall man. They seemed to be getting along well, and he hoped it meant good things for her. She deserved an easy life, and hopefully, love. Mery's father had died years earlier, and she'd been focused on him and his siblings since then. Now that she had the opportunity, he hoped she would have more.

He finally managed to sneak into a side hallway. There were still people here, but fewer of them, and most were too busy to pay attention to him. He briskly walked past them, headed to his rooms. The party could continue without him.

"You're running away," a voice said.

Mery smiled and turned to look at Sed. "Wouldn't you? I hate this." Sed was the only person Mery could be entirely honest with, except for one thing—his feelings.

Sed nodded. "I can't say I enjoy this kind of party. You're the guest of honor, though. People will look for you."

"I don't care. I've had enough."

"Is it because Ibuki introduced you to the future queen?"

Mery grimaced and looked around, but no one was listening to them. "How do you know who she was?"

"I asked around. She's the prime minister's niece."

"That's why you think she'll be the future queen?"

"I don't think she will be, but Ibuki and the prime minister seem to."

"I think that's why Ibuki introduce her to me."

"Have you told him you're not going to marry her?"

"No. I just stood up and left."

Sed laughed. The sound was enough for Mery to relax. It

shouldn't be, and he knew this was going to be a huge problem if Sed stuck around, but he wasn't going to be, so Mery allowed himself to bask in his feelings and admit them to himself.

He was falling in love with a god. Sed was nothing like what Mery had imagined gods would be like. He was more like a human, which no doubt was the reason Mery felt drawn to him. It didn't hurt that Sed was gorgeous, too.

"I'm sure Ibuki was shocked," Sed said.

"Probably, but I didn't stick around to find out. He'll find me soon enough anyway."

"Remember that you don't have to do anything you don't want to."

Mery sighed. "I wish it was the truth. Who's going to stand up for me once you're gone, though?"

"You should stand up for yourself, but don't worry. I'm not going anywhere anytime soon."

Mery didn't want to hope yet. "What does that mean? Your job here is done, isn't it? I'm officially king."

"And I'm the protector of kingship. I'm not just here for the coronation ceremony. I'm here to protect you for as long as you need me to."

Mery wished it meant more, but he would have to make do with this. "Thank you. I don't know what I would have done if you hadn't been there for me."

"You won't have to find out."

Not yet, anyway. One day, though, Sed would leave, and Mery would stay. He supposed he should take advantage of the time they still had together. It would make it even harder when Sed finally left, but Mery was used to hardship.

He'd given up everything when he'd agreed to be king. Nothing would happen with Sed, but Mery wanted them to at least be friends. That was the one thing he wanted for himself, the one thing that didn't have anything to do with him being king. In this, he wanted to be selfish and think only of himself.

Sed could see Mery didn't believe him, and he didn't blame him. He'd been talking about going back home since he'd arrived, and while he did miss his old life, he wasn't willing to sacrifice Mery's safety to go back to it. He was a god. Even if he stayed here until Mery passed away of old age, it would feel like mere minutes to him.

But the world would be different in sixty years. Sed had a lot to think about, and he wasn't ready to do it yet.

"I'll walk you to your rooms," he told Mery.

Mery nodded. "Thank you. You don't have to if you'd rather go back to the party, though."

"I'd rather not. I might have to talk to my mother again, and it's the last thing I want."

His words made Mery chuckle. "I'm not sure I understand what you have going on with your mother. I love mine, and I wish I could spend more time with her."

They started walking down the hallway. "I love my mother, too," Sed explained. "But I was born thousands of years ago, and she still tries to control my life. I would be more eager to spend time with her if she just let me do what I want."

"I see. Well, my mother never tried to control my life, but now, many other people are."

"It's something you learn to deal with. You're young for a king, and it's understandable that you're not sure what to do or say. You'll grow into it." If he was given a chance. Sed would do everything he could to make sure he was, but he couldn't be everywhere at once, and he couldn't stay with Mery all the time.

He had to find out what was happening and stop it, and

while he had a good idea of who was behind it, it wouldn't be easy.

"I hope you're right. I don't want to spend the next fifty years having to do whatever Ibuki tells me to do."

"You don't have to do what he tells you to do. He's your personal assistant. If anything, he should be doing what *you* want him to do."

Mery shrugged. "I know. It's not easy to go from being a farmer to being this," he said, gesturing at the palace around them.

"I understand, and I think you'll get over it eventually."

Mery's smile was hesitant. "And you'll help me?"

"As much as I can. I promised, and I try not to go back on my promises." Too many gods did.

Too many gods did awful things to humans just because they wanted to and because they could. Sed couldn't say he was entirely innocent, but he always tried not to hurt anyone, not even humans. It had become easier once he viewed both gods and humans the same way.

They walked until they reached the door of Mery's rooms. He pressed a hand against it, hesitant, then turned to look at Sed. "Would you like to come in?"

Sed looked at the guards that stood on both sides of the doors. "Did you need anything?"

Mery caught Sed's gaze. "I just wanted to talk about the ceremony."

Sed could tell it was a lie, but he went along with it. "Of course."

Mery walked in, with Sed following him and closing the door behind him. Mery's stance changed as soon as they were alone. His shoulders slumped, and his back relaxed. He looked even more tired than he had in the hallway. He rubbed his face and gave Sed a tired smile. "Thanks for all of this. I needed to get away, but I'm not sure I want to be alone right now."

"Do you want me to call anyone? Maybe your mother?"

Mery hesitated. "I do want to see her, but not right now. She's having fun, and I don't want her to have to take care of me. I'm an adult, after all."

"I don't think she would care."

"Probably not. But it's been a long time since I needed her to take care of me, and I don't want to start again now. This is something I have to deal with on my own, unfortunately."

"I disagree. You have a lot of people around you, and while most are working against you, you have some on your side, too."

After sitting down, Mery started taking off the jewels that adorned his body. He dropped them onto a small table next to the couch as if he didn't care, and he probably didn't. Sed had learned the first time they met that Mery didn't care about some aspects of being king. He didn't want the power or the money or anything like that. He just wanted to keep his family safe.

"I don't want to pull my family into whatever is happening. I'm doing this for them, and pulling them into the situation would put them in danger. I can't afford for that to happen," Mery said.

"I understand. Qebui and I are on your side, too. If you ever need anything, whatever it is, let one of us know. We'll do everything we can to help."

Mery was finally done with the jewels, and without them, he looked a little more like himself. Sed found himself wanting to reach for him and touch his skin, but he kept his hands to himself.

"You know, you keep repeating it," Mery said.

Sed frowned. "Repeating what?"

"That you're here to help me. What am I giving you in exchange, though?"

Sed shook his head and went to sit next to Mery. "You don't have to give me anything. I'm not doing this so you'll owe me. I'm doing it because you need help and protection, and as a god, it's easy for me to provide them to you."

"I guess I don't understand why. Since I met you, you never stopped talking about your life in the United States and how eager you are to go back to it. Now, you told me you're staying here, and I know it's for my sake. I don't want you to have to give up anything. You shouldn't have to. It's not your job."

Technically it was, since he was the protector of kingship and the king. He wasn't here because it was his job, though, not anymore. He didn't want to lie to Mery, and he didn't want Mery to think he was in this only because he had to. "I like you," he said. The words felt blunt coming out of his mouth, but he'd learned a long time ago to go straight to the point and avoid dancing around issues. It saved time and made everything easier.

Mery looked startled. "You do?"

"I've liked you since the first time we met. I expected someone who was in this only for the power and the money, but nothing could be further from the truth. You're a good person, and you're trying to do the right thing for everyone but yourself. If you won't think about your safety and your happiness, someone else has to, and why not me?"

Sed wanted much more than Mery's safety, but he didn't dare say it out loud. He wasn't blind, and after spending so much time with Mery in the past few weeks, he suspected Mery felt the same way. Mery was the king, though, and he was still dealing with what that meant. He was still learning what he could and couldn't do, and Sed wasn't about to push him either way, especially considering what he was.

When Mery didn't answer, Sed smiled and resisted the urge to kiss him. "I should probably go," he said, starting to get to his feet.

Mery caught his wrist, stopping him. "I'd like you to stay," he said, his voice slightly rough.

Sed sucked in a breath. "Of course."

Mery stared. "But I need you to understand what I'm asking." He took a deep breath and straightened his back. "I'm not sure what you meant when you said you liked me, but I can tell you what I mean when I say that I like you. I realize you're a god and probably don't care about human emotions, but I want something for myself for once. I want to forget about being king and just be Mery. I want something no one can take away from me."

And apparently, he wanted Sed to give him that something.

Mery tried to forget the fear that gripped his stomach and pulled so Sed would sit next to him again. Once he had, Mery swung his leg to the side and straddled Sed. He held his breath, half expecting Sed to ask what he was doing or to throw him to the floor. Instead, Sed's hands gripped Mery's hips as if trying to keep him there.

Mery swallowed. Sed's eyes were wide, but he wasn't moving or trying to move Mery, which had to be a good thing. Sed still didn't move when Mery hooked his arms around his neck or when he leaned closer, only stopping when their lips brushed against each other.

He could feel Sed's breath on his skin, but he hesitated anyway.

Sed closed the distance between them. His lips were soft and gentle, and Mery sighed in relief and pleasure and opened his mouth.

Sed didn't hesitate, plunging his tongue inside, stroking Mery's, driving him crazy.

Mery wanted more. He felt like with Sed, nothing would ever be enough. He wanted him too much, but he supposed a kiss was a good start. He didn't know if they were both ready or willing for more, and he wasn't going to push, but gods, he wanted it.

Mery slid his hands down Sed's back, then his sides. He hesitated before slipping them around his waist and touching the small of his back. He was wearing a traditional skirt like Mery, although he looked much more gorgeous and elegant than Mery could ever hope to be. He would have refused the skirt if he hadn't known the gods expected him to look like the pharaohs had.

One thing that was great with the skirt was the easy access it gave him to Sed's body. Mery could feel Sed's muscles ripple under his touch, and when he pushed a fingertip under the seam of the skirt, just enough to brush against the top of Sed's ass cheek, Sed groaned and thrust forward.

They were both hard. The knowledge would have made Mery's mouth go dry if he and Sed hadn't still been kissing. But they were, and Mery never wanted to stop, not even to get naked. He didn't even know if Sed wanted that or if they'd continue kissing until it was time for Sed to go.

Mery was not going to think about that tonight, though.

Since Sed was still kissing him and not protesting, Mery pushed both his hands under Sed's skirt. Sed jerked, but Mery felt him smile against his lips. He wanted this as much as Mery, which was a relief.

Mery flexed his fingers. Just like he'd thought, Sed's ass felt perfect against his palms. It was round and bouncy, sprinkled with hair that made Mery's skin tingle.

But he wanted more.

He tore his mouth away from Sed's, wanting to ask for whatever Sed was ready to give him. Before he could, Sed kissed his jaw, then his neck.

Mery shuddered and tilted his head to give Sed easier access. Sed lightly bit Mery's neck, and at the same time, Mery felt his hands slide up his thighs and under his skirt.

Unfortunately, he was wearing a pair of modern boxer-briefs under the skirt, which meant he would have to get up if he wanted to get naked. Sed didn't seem to mind or care, and he pushed his fingers under the soft fabric. His fingertips brushed against the sensitive skin where thigh met groin, then the side of Mery's balls.

Mery squeaked and pushed his hips forward. Sed chuckled and raised his head to look at Mery. His cheeks were flushed and his lips glistened, and Mery thought he'd never looked so beautiful.

"What do you want?" Sed asked.

Mery didn't know how to answer. Could he tell Sed he wanted everything? He wasn't even sure what that everything was. He just knew that he didn't want Sed to leave and that he wanted to keep kissing him.

Sed smiled gently when Mery didn't answer. "Have you ever done this with a man?"

Mery rolled his eyes. "With a man, yes. With a god, no." Although even when he'd had sex with guys, it was nothing like this. It was rushed and tinged with a hint of shame and so much fear that they'd be seen.

Mery didn't have to be afraid with Sed, though. Sed was a god, and no one would even think about saying anything about him being with a man. But no one would see them tonight. They were in Mery's rooms, and while the guards might realize something was going on, Mery didn't care.

"I might be a god, but it doesn't make me any different from the other men you've been with," Sed said.

"It's not that. I want you so much, but I'm afraid you don't." Mery didn't feel better now that the words were out.

Sed's expression shifted again. "I want you. How do you

not see it?"

"I think it's easy not to see it when I'm not used to it."

Sed kissed Mery again. He retrieved his hands from under Mery's skirt, put them on his ass, and rose to his feet. Mery didn't hesitate to wrap his legs around Sed's waist. He didn't think Sed would drop him, but he wanted to be as close to him as possible. Sed moved, hopefully headed toward Mery's bedroom. Mery didn't check — that was how much he trusted Sed.

Sed didn't dump him onto the bed when they reached it. Instead, he kneeled on the edge of the mattress and lowered him down gently. He hovered over him, their lips only inches apart, as if he wasn't sure what to do. Mery wasn't, either, but he knew what he wanted, and he'd had enough of fear and loneliness. Even if nothing happened between them beyond this, he didn't want to stop. He'd been protecting his heart for a long time, and while falling in love with a god probably wasn't the brightest idea, he couldn't ignore how he felt or what he wanted.

He reached down, thankful he'd already taken off the jewels he'd had to wear for the ceremony and the party. It made it easier for him to open the skirt, then push his underwear down his thighs. It couldn't go down far, since Sed had caged Mery's legs with his own, but it was enough to free Mery's aching cock.

The tip brushed against Sed's naked stomach. Mery shivered and watched as Sed peered down to look at it. He reached between their bodies, catching Mery's cock with his hand, wrapping his long fingers around it, and gently stroking.

Mery groaned and closed his eyes. He tried to open his legs, but he was stuck, no matter how hard he tried. When Sed chuckled, he glared at him.

"Why are you torturing me?" he asked.

"If anything, I'm torturing both of us. Don't you think I want to spread your legs and fuck you right now?"

Mery's cheeks heated. No one had ever talked to him that way, and while he should feel embarrassed, he couldn't, not when he was with Sed. "Do it," he said in a throaty voice.

Sed stared at him for a second. Then he finally moved, sliding down Mery's legs and hooking his thumbs into Mery's underwear. He pulled them down slowly, staring at the skin he was revealing. Mery wanted to tell him to hurry, but he was starting to see that Sed only did what he wanted, even in bed.

As soon as Mery's legs were free, he rolled to his stomach, snatched the lube from his nightstand, and opened his legs. He could imagine what Sed was seeing, and while there was a curl of embarrassment in his stomach, he also felt sexy. He didn't often feel that way, but when he twisted his head around to look at Sed, it blossomed into heat. Sed was staring as if he'd never seen anything so mesmerizing, and while Mery was sure that wasn't the case, it pleased him.

He pulled himself onto his knees and opened the lube. The movement seemed to spur Sed into moving, and he reached for his own white skirt. It hung low on his hips, and Mery couldn't look away as he opened it.

Mery almost dropped the lube when Sed's cock was revealed. It was hard, slightly curved to the right, and it looked like it would fill him perfectly. He couldn't wait for that to happen, and he opened the lube, squeezing too much of it on his fingers. He didn't care. He dumped the lube onto the bed and reached behind himself, looking at Sed again.

He was tracking every one of Mery's movements, and his eyes flared when Mery's fingers found his hole. He was used to this—he had done it just last night while thinking about Sed—so he started right away with two fingers, pushing them inside his body and groaning at the burning stretch. It would feel even better when Sed was the one stretching him, but in the meantime, this was good enough.

Mery felt Sed move behind him. The mattress dipped, and he felt Sed's warmth behind him. It was soothing but also exciting, especially when Sed's palms landed on Mery's ass. He pulled the cheeks apart, and Mery had to look back.

Sed was staring at the spot where Mery's fingers were moving in and out of his ass. His lips were slightly parted, and his cheeks were flushed. His hair was messed up from where Mery's fingers had dug into it earlier, and it framed his face perfectly. Mery wanted to mess it up even more.

He screwed his eyes shut when a finger that didn't belong to him pushed into his ass alongside his. He and Sed moved together for a few moments. Then when Mery pulled his fingers out, Sed batted them away. Mery expected him to take over the task of prepping him, and he did, but not the way Mery thought he would.

The swipe of a hot, wet tongue over his hole made him jerk forward. Sed seemed to have expected it, because he let go of one of Mery's ass cheeks and grabbed his hip with it, pulling him back as he continued licking him. Mery almost screamed when Sed's tongue pushed inside his hole. The only reason he didn't was that he didn't want the guards to come running, so he bit onto his pillow as Sed continued rimming him.

No one had ever done this to Mery. He'd known about it, but he'd never imagined it would feel this good. He was panting and humping the mattress by the time he felt Sed pull away. Sed used his hands to pull Mery's hips upward, and when Mery felt the head of Sed's cock push against his hole, he tilted his hips. He was more than ready for Sed to fuck him. He'd probably come as soon as Sed was inside of him.

But Sed moved frustratingly slowly. He kept Mery from slamming back against him with his hands on Mery's lips. Once he was fully inside Mery, Mery took a deep breath, then another. By the time he was done, Sed was finally fucking him, and it was everything Mery had ever wanted.

Sed was strong but not forceful, and his thrusts were smooth. Mery buried his face against his pillow as their movements pushed him toward the headboard. He would have to grab it soon, but for now, he was at Sed's mercy, completely his and not caring.

This was what he wanted. He was king during the day, but during the night — with Sed — he was just Mery. He was Mery who allowed Sed to fuck him and loved it. He was Mery who'd lost his heart to a god and didn't want it back.

"You're the most beautiful man I've ever seen," Sed murmured. At the same time, he reached down for Mery's cock, wrapping his fingers around it and pulling every time he buried himself inside of him.

Mery came with a sob. He felt loved and cherished, even though it might all be an illusion. He didn't care right now, and he didn't want to know what this meant for Sed. As he felt Sed come inside him, he focused on how gentle Sed was and how he made him feel. That was all that mattered for tonight.

Reality was inescapable, and it would hit Mery upside the head soon enough. For now, Mery was just a man, and he was loved.

CHAPTER FIVE

M ery was finally working the way he should have since he'd arrived. He didn't know how Sed had managed, but the prime minister had come to see him in his office the day after the coronation ceremony, and even though he'd obviously been reluctant, they'd sat down and had gone over what Mery could do and what he still needed to learn. It felt like a huge step forward, and while it meant Mery had more work than ever, it felt good to be doing something, especially when that something was what he'd been chosen for.

He eyed the pile of documents on the side of his desk. This time, they had nothing to do with food and wine or a party. These were all things he needed to read and learn if he wanted to be able to do his job. He'd been relieved to find out he wouldn't have to do it on his own, since he had a prime minister and other ministers to help him, but he didn't fully trust them, and he wanted to do as much as he could on his own.

Thankfully, he had *other* people helping him, too. He and Sed were closer than ever, and Mery hoped that never changed, even though he knew it was pointless. There were also Jimmy and Qebui, and while they weren't in this for the same reason Sed was, they were friendly enough, and Mery had started spending most of his evenings with them and Sed. It was nothing like the life he'd left behind, but he was beginning to realize it didn't have to be. He could be happy in many ways, and maybe he could be happy as a king, too.

A knock on the door made him groan. He sat up straighter, schooled his expression, and called out, "Yes?"

The door opened, and Ibuki looked in. "Your highness? The prime minister is here for your meeting."

"Let him in, please."

Mery had known the prime minister would come around, and while he wished he could avoid this meeting, he knew better than to try. It would make Ibuki and the prime minister all too happy to see him going back to the old days when he didn't know what was happening, and they could do whatever they wanted behind his back.

The prime minister walked in. Mery watched him as he came closer and tried not to grimace. He never looked forward to time spent with the prime minister, but he supposed he should get used to it. The man wasn't going anywhere, and neither was Mery.

"Your highness," the prime minister said.

Mery forced himself to smile. "Ouser. How are you doing this morning?"

"All good, all good. Well, my back hurts, but that's what happens when you get old."

"I suppose I'll find out soon enough."

The prime minister snorted. "You're not even in your mid-twenties. It'll take a while for you to find out." He looked straight at Mery. "Ready to start?"

Mery nodded. "What's on the schedule today?"

For a few hours, Mery listened to the prime minister talk about neighboring countries and the relationships they had with them. The prime minister didn't like a few of those, but Mery couldn't tell why. He would have to find out in other ways, because he doubted the prime minister would answer truthfully if he asked.

It was a lot to listen to and even more to learn, but Mery was taking notes, and he knew he could do this. He had to because it was his job now, and he intended to do it the right way.

He was grateful when the prime minister decided it was time to take a break. He called out for the servants to bring food and drinks and leaned back in his chair.

Mery still found it awkward to rely on servants, but in a way, it made his life easier. He was uncomfortable with the thought of people doing his laundry and bringing him food when he could get on his feet and go fetch it by himself, but he knew that if he tried, people would be outraged, and the servants would feel like he didn't need them. He might not, but this was what they were paid for, and he wanted to allow them to do their job.

"How are you doing, your majesty?" the prime minister asked.

"It's a lot to take in, and it'll probably take me a few days to digest everything you just told me, but I'll wrap my head around it eventually."

The prime minister nodded. "I understand. I've been doing this most of my life, so of course, it feels easy to me. You know you can come to me if you need anything."

He kept repeating that, but Mery didn't think he meant it the way Mery might if he said the same thing. Mery could go to him if he needed help, but he would probably have to give up something in exchange, and when it came to the prime minister, that something was bound to be power.

The servants came in with tea and pastries. They put everything down onto a small table in the corner, and Mery and the prime minister headed that way. It felt good to sit on the couch and not be as tense as he'd been that morning, but the meeting wasn't over yet.

The prime minister ate a few pastries before he casually mentioned his niece. "I saw you and Aneksi talking at the party after your coronation ceremony," he said.

Mery almost cringed. "Briefly, yes. Ibuki introduced me to her."

"I hope the two of you got along well."

"I suppose we did." For the two minutes they'd talked anyway.

"Good, good. I haven't mentioned it yet, your majesty, but you ought to make a decision about your marriage soon. The sooner you have an heir, the better it will be for the country."

And surely, Mery would want to do everything he could for the country. It was implied, and Mery didn't like it, but he couldn't deny Ouser was right. Like always when it came to the prime minister, the words were self-serving. He wanted Mery to choose his niece as a bride so he could be closer to the throne. He wasn't saying it out loud, but Mery wasn't an idiot.

"What would happen if I didn't have an heir?" Mery asked.

The prime minister's eyes went wide. "Why shouldn't you? You're young, and you'll be able to father many children."

"I might not want children." And he certainly didn't want to get married, especially not to the prime minister's niece.

"That might have been possible when you were a farmer, your majesty, but as the king, it's one of your duties to the country."

"The gods could choose someone else if I died without an heir. It's what they did when they found me, after all."

"But it's not how things were done in the past."

"It doesn't mean we can't change them. I'm sure you're not happy at being pushed to the side to make space for me, a farmer who doesn't know what he's talking about."

The prime minister looked offended. "If I have ever said or done anything that gave you that impression, your majesty—"

"You didn't. I understand what you're saying about me having a duty toward the country, but I'm not willing to give up my entire life for this."

"You wouldn't be giving up anything. You're going to get

married eventually anyway."

Mery wasn't about to tell him why he'd never thought he would get married, but he shook his head. "Having a wife has never crossed my mind, and it still doesn't. I'm not convinced it's necessary, and even if it is, I don't want to rush things. I don't wish to get married just because I have to, but rather because I want to. I'm sure you can understand that. Don't you want your niece to have a husband she loves rather than having to marry someone she barely knows?"

The prime minister looked offended and like he didn't know how to answer.

Mery enjoyed it. He was finally starting to realize that even though he didn't know what being a king meant, he *was* the king, and he had a say in what happened, especially when it involved his personal life.

He wasn't ready to give up Sed. He didn't know how long Sed would stick around, but Mery wasn't giving him up one second sooner than he had to. He especially wasn't giving him up to marry a woman he didn't know just to please people he didn't like.

Sed was in the gardens, one of his favorite places to spend time in the palace, when Anhur found him. He'd expected the god of war to want to talk to him eventually, if anything, to find out why he was poking around. He was relieved he wouldn't have to go after the other god himself.

He didn't think Anhur was aware of what was going on. He probably thought Sed was curious, not that Sed had realized he was up to something and was trying to find out what it was. Hopefully, that would help Sed find more details about what Anhur and the prime minister were planning.

"So this is where you're hiding," Anhur said, looking around.

"Not hiding. Merely spending time."

Anhur was wearing the traditional white skirt the ancient Egyptians had worn, which was telling. Anhur's shoulders were broad, and he sported a mulish expression. Sed wondered if he was here to try to scare him away. If that was the case, he was about to get a nasty surprise.

"I don't see the appeal," Anhur said.

"Well, life is good because it's varied, isn't it? Things would be boring if we all enjoyed the same things."

Anhur nodded curtly. "Which is why I'm curious as to why you're still here. From what I know, you were enjoying your life as a human."

Sed didn't know who had told Anhur about that, but he wasn't surprised someone had. It was well-known in his family that he didn't enjoy spending time with other gods but would rather spend time with humans. "I still am. I can enjoy life both here and in the United States."

"Don't you want to go back? I mean, you left because you didn't want to be here. Why would you want to stick around now?"

Sed had to force himself not to smile. He was pretty sure he looked like an idiot, but then, that was what he was aiming for. He wanted Anhur to view him as harmless. "Well, I've been away from home for many years," he began. "Even though I was happy in the United States, I never realized how much I missed this place. No matter how eager I was to leave, it's still home. Besides, there's my mother to deal with. She's been trying to convince me to come home for decades, and she's so happy I finally obeyed that she won't let me go back. I think that staying here for a few years will help soothe her, and I'll be able to do what I want again once she is."

Anhur looked worried for a moment. He tried to school his expression, but Sed had already seen it. "You shouldn't let your mother tell you what to do."

"I'm sure that a god of war like you doesn't, but it's not in my nature to fight people, and especially not my mother. You know who she is. I don't fancy feeling the sharpness of her arrows."

Even though it had been thousands of years since Sed's mother had had to protect Egypt, it had been her role once. She'd protected the south frontier by killing their country's enemies with her sharp arrows, and she was still freakishly good with a bow. She'd never hurt Sed with them, but Anhur probably didn't know that.

"Be that as it may, she shouldn't have a say in your life."

Sed wanted to smack Anhur, but instead, he tightened his hands into fists and hoped they were hidden well enough that Anhur wouldn't see how angry he was. "She doesn't, not really. Like I explained, I'm not staying just for her. I missed this place, and I want to spend time here before going back. I don't see how it's your problem or why you're worried about it."

"I'm not worried," Anhur said in a rush. "I was just wondering what was happening."

"I see." Sed did. Anhur didn't give two shits about him. He just wanted to find out why Sed was still around and if he was going to be a threat to whatever he and the prime minister were plotting.

He was. Sed had every intention to put himself between them and Mery. He would have even if he and Mery hadn't been together, but now that they were, he would sacrifice anything to keep Mery safe.

There was nothing he could do when it came to pulling Mery away from being the king anymore. Mery had made his decision, and Sed would never have tried to stop him from accepting the crown. Since Mery was the king, albeit unwillingly, the next best thing Sed could do was make sure he was respected as such, and that included squashing any kind of revolt or plot against him.

Mery wasn't a bad king. He wasn't a good one yet, but he was working hard, and Sed couldn't wait until that happened. Mery would have a glorious future, and even though he'd never meant to be king, he was dealing with this the best way he could. He wanted the best for the country, if not for himself, and Sed wouldn't allow anyone to intervene. If one day Mery started caring more about himself and his happiness than about being king, Sed would say something. For now, there wasn't a need for him or anyone else to do so.

"Did you need anything else?" he asked Anhur.

The god shook his head. "I was just curious."

"It's always good to have another god to chat with. That's one more thing I missed when I was living with humans."

Anhur's only answer was to grunt and walk away.

Sed watched him leave, wondering what the next step would be. Anhur didn't strike him as extremely intelligent, but he was a god, which meant he was dangerous even if he wasn't. The fact that he was working with two humans who wanted nothing more than power and money and had a finite amount of time to get them made him even more dangerous.

Sed had no doubt that the prime minister and Anhur would eventually make their move. Sed didn't know what that move would be yet, and he might not find out until it happened, but he had to be careful. He would never forgive himself if something happened to Mery. He would also never forgive Anhur for it, and as a god, he could hold a grudge for thousands of years.

Chapter Six

Mery ducked around the corner when he saw the prime minister coming toward him. Ever since he'd told Ouser that he wasn't planning on getting married or having children, the man had been hounding him to change his mind. Sometimes, he even dragged his niece along, and Mery wasn't in the mood to have to listen to another one of his tirades, especially not if Aneksi was present.

Mery had expected her to be as annoyed as he was at her uncle's behavior, but she often looked at him like he was a juicy steak, and it made him uncomfortable.

"Ouser!" a male voice boomed.

Mery was close enough to hear the conversation, and while he'd been planning on sneaking away before the prime minister could notice him, he stayed where he was.

"Don't yell," Ouser hissed. "We can't afford for anyone to see us together."

"Bah. I'm a god. You should be honored to be seen with Anhur, the powerful god of war."

Mery rolled his eyes. He knew who Anhur was thanks to Sed, and while he might be the god of war, he was a minor god that only a few people remembered. It was a miracle he showed his face around the palace. From what Mery knew, gods wanted to be remembered, so maybe Anhur was shoving himself into as many people's lives as he could so he'd get recognition.

That probably was why he was also plotting something with the prime minister.

"And I am," Ouser said. "It's still not a good idea for people to realize we know each other. There's a lot at stake here."

"Don't you think I know that? You're not giving me what you promised, and I'm getting impatient."

"You knew it would take a while for all of this to slot into place. Once Aneksi is married to the king and pregnant with a boy, we can move ahead with our plan."

"Sed isn't leaving like we thought he would. He says he missed this place, but I don't believe him. He thinks he's better than us, and I see right through him. He's plotting something."

"He won't be able to stop us."

"You're sure? Because he's been spending a lot of time with the king. He's probably the reason you haven't managed to get results yet."

"I don't think he is. I've been pushing for the king to build more temples, including one for you, of course. But the king isn't used to having so many responsibilities, and he doesn't understand how important it is for him to put the country first. He still foolishly believes he should marry for love, which is why he hasn't agreed to marry Aneksi yet. But he will. I'll make sure of it."

Mery wondered how the prime minister was planning on doing that. He hadn't been about to say yes even before, but now that he knew the prime minister was working against him with a minor god, there were even fewer incentives for him to do so. He had a hard time believing that the only thing Anhur would get out of this was a temple, but maybe he didn't know gods as well as he thought he did. Sed was one of a kind, and it wouldn't be surprising to find out other gods wanted power and to be adored more than he did.

Mery decided he'd heard enough. He could probably learn more about the plans if he continued listening in, but he was afraid someone would notice him. He was lucky no servant or guard had passed through the hallway yet. They would eventually, and he wasn't willing to risk it, especially since it looked like the prime minister was trying to find him to once again push his niece on to him.

He turned around, walking the opposite way from where the prime minister and the guards were standing. He snuck out into the garden, needing some time to wrap his mind around what he heard and what it might mean for him.

He wasn't about to say yes to marrying Aneksi, but what would the prime minister do if he continued resisting? At this point, Mery wouldn't put it past him to find a way around it, and Mery didn't know if he would be able to resist. He could say no as many times as he wanted, but if the prime minister came up with a law that said the king had to be married for the good of the country, would Mery be able to continue saying no?

Mery had to think. But to do that, he needed time and space without anyone wanting to talk to him. The best place to find that was his private garden, so he headed there, hiding behind trees and bushes so no one would notice him. He was relieved when he reached the stone bench that he'd been spending more and more time on. It was empty, which wasn't surprising since it was located in his private garden, but sometimes Jimmy was there. He wasn't today, and Mery sat on the hard surface, closing his eyes and taking a deep breath.

He knew what he wanted to do and what he didn't want. Was there a way to get out of this marriage? Maybe if he was in a relationship, he could convince the prime minister he shouldn't marry anyone he didn't want, but he wasn't sure where he and Sed stood. They'd had sex, and they were friendly enough, but they hadn't talked about what it meant. Mery had been afraid to ask, and Sed hadn't volunteered any kind of information.

Where did that leave Mery? He wanted so much more than

what he and Sed already had. He realized it was selfish to ask Sed to leave his life behind to stay with him. Besides, Sed was a man. He couldn't give Mery children, not as far as Mery knew. Some gods who presented as male had carried babies, but Mery doubted Sed was one of them.

Was a pregnancy the only way to get an heir? Mery had never thought much about it. When he'd been a farmer, he'd known he would never get married and have children with a woman, and he hadn't been rich enough to consider other options. Now, he was, and the thought of adopting a child who needed it was appealing. Mery was nowhere near ready to do it, not at twenty-three and when he'd only just started working as the king and understanding what it meant. One day, though, he would do it.

He didn't know if Sed would be with him when it happened.

They had to talk. It was the only way to find out what was going on between them and if Mery should keep his hopes up when it came to a relationship with Sed. He was afraid it was too much to ask, but he was starting to realize that his fear didn't mean he couldn't ask questions. He needed to get over how awkward he felt all the time and act like a king.

Sed wasn't one of Mery's subjects. He could do whatever he wanted, and, knowing him, he wouldn't have a problem telling Mery how he felt. Maybe knowing for sure would help Mery feel better and make better decisions. He already knew he didn't want to marry anyone, least of all the prime minister's niece, but it would help to know he wasn't alone. Feeling secure in his relationship with Sed felt like a priority, but it was also terrifying.

What if Sed didn't want the same as Mery? What if what was between them was just sex and he didn't wish for anything more? Would he leave if Mery asked? It would be his right, but he'd promised Mery he would stick around and help him. Mery had to trust Sed would keep his word. He had to trust Sed like he had until now and remember that so far, Sed hadn't betrayed him and hadn't made promises he hadn't kept.

Sed was amused. Mery hadn't seen him when he'd walked into the garden and made a beeline for his favorite bench. Sed hadn't meant it to happen, but it gave him the opportunity to look at the man he was in love with unguarded.

It didn't happen often. Mery had quickly learned to keep his feelings and thoughts to himself in the palace, and Sed suspected he did it with him, too. They hadn't talked about what was going on between them or what they wanted it to be, but they'd have to. It was difficult to read Mery and guess what he wanted from Sed, though, and Sed wasn't used to that.

Even though he'd been living with humans for decades, he'd never felt as vulnerable and as close to being one as he did now.

He understood better how Jimmy had felt when he dated. Sed couldn't remember wanting anyone as much as he wanted Mery, and the thought that Mery might not feel the same way made his stomach churn. It would be better for both of them if feelings weren't involved and if they stayed away from each other's beds, but it was too late for that. Hopefully, it wouldn't become a disaster, because Sed had no intention of leaving Mery unless Mery asked him.

Maybe he would, but maybe he wouldn't, and there was only one way for Sed to find out.

He stepped away from the tree he'd been leaning against. Mery still didn't notice him, so he cleared his throat, chuckling when Mery jumped off the bench and looked around like he expected to be attacked. Maybe he did. Things were tense in the palace, no matter how hard Sed tried to shield Mery from it.

"What are you doing hiding on your bench?" he asked as he walked closer.

Mery huffed and sat back down. "Exactly that. I'm hiding."

"Do you want company?"

Mery hesitated, so Sed expected him to say no. Instead, he nodded and patted the bench next to him. Sed couldn't resist and kissed Mery's cheek once he'd sat down, smiling at how flustered that small gesture made Mery.

"What are you hiding from?" he asked. Not him, clearly, but he had to know if he was going to keep Mery safe.

Mery sighed and leaned against Sed. "The prime minister and Ibuki. I swear, it's almost as if I work for them instead of the other way around. They both keep pushing their agendas on me, and I hate it. How many times will I have to tell them I'm not planning on marrying anyone any time soon, but especially not a woman I barely know?"

Sed wrapped his arm around Mery's shoulders. "I'm sorry."

Mery shrugged. "It's not your fault."

"It's not, but I wish there was more I could do for you."

"I doubt anything would stop them except for me marrying someone else."

Sed had the wild thought of offering himself in marriage, but he kept the words in. Now wasn't the time, not when they hadn't yet talked about what was going on between them.

"By the way, I heard the prime minister talking with Anhur in the hallway," Mery continued.

That was enough to pull Sed's attention back from thoughts of marriage. "What were they saying?"

"Apparently, Ouser told Anhur he'd have a temple built in his honor or something. That's why he wants me to marry Aneksi—so he'll be able to influence and manipulate me even more. And I think you were right when you said that if I don't go along with it, they'll eventually get rid of me. Ouser said that everything would be easier once Aneksi and I are married and she's pregnant with a boy."

The conversation made Sed's blood boil, even though he was hearing it second hand. How dare anyone plan on killing Mery when he was trying to do the right thing? And even if he wasn't, he didn't deserve to die, especially not so the prime minister could keep his power.

Mery straightened and twisted around to face Sed. "What would the gods do if I were to die?"

"I believe they would look at your heir to take your place, not only on the throne but also as their messenger. If your heir is still a child, then either your wife or the prime minister would step in."

Mery nodded. He didn't look surprised, and Sed wasn't, either. "So that's what they're aiming for. Do you think they thought about it themselves, or did Anhur influence them?"

That was a difficult question to answer. "Gods are generally good manipulators, but I don't think the prime minister would have agreed to this if he didn't want to do it. He's angry because he had all the power until you were thrust on the scene and he had to take a step back and let you take the lead."

Mery snorted. "As if. He's been teaching me, but I'm not an idiot. I know he's trying to make me do what he thinks should be done. I've stood up to him several times, and he wasn't happy, but I'm still not in full control."

The easiest way to change that would be to get rid of the prime minister, but Sed was wary of doing that. They knew Ouser and what he was planning. If they fired him, someone else would eventually take his place, and they'd have to find out what was happening again. Sed would rather deal with the devil they already knew than a new one, at least for now. If the prime minister really was plotting to eliminate the king, he'd have to pay for it eventually, but it was too soon.

"Maybe I should go along with it," Mery said.

Sed frowned, wondering if he'd missed part of the conversation. "Go along with what?"

"Everything. I never wanted to be king, and I still don't. It would be easier if Ouser were still in charge, and that's what he wants. I could let him make the decisions and be king only by name. I might not even have to marry his niece if I do that."

Sed understood why the thought was appealing to Mery, and he wanted to agree. Mery didn't want the kind of responsibilities that came along with being king, and he'd been pushed into it.

But he *had* agreed. He hadn't had to, but now, he was king, and he couldn't just step back and allow this to happen, no matter how tempting it was. "Is that what you really want?" Sed asked.

Mery sighed. "No. I knew what I was doing when I agreed to be king, and I want this to work. I might not have wanted it, but it doesn't change the fact that I'm king, and I can't ignore that. I'm just not sure what to do and how to deal with Ouser, and I'm scared of what he might do if I continue pushing back against him."

There were many things Sed wanted to tell Mery, but instead, he reached for him and pulled him into his arms. Mery squeaked and resisted for a moment, but then he gave in and became pliant in Sed's arms. Sed kissed him, trying to make Mery forget about anything but them but also to tell him how much he cared and to remind him that he was here.

Sed's decision had already been made. Even if Mery didn't want him the same way he wanted Mery, he wouldn't leave. Mery needed him, and Sed couldn't abandon him. If it meant he had to stay away from Pittsburgh and the States for the rest of Mery's life, that he had to hide in the celestial palace to keep an eye on him from a distance, he'd do it.

But first, he had to know what Mery wanted. There was still a chance he'd want to be with Sed, and if that was the case, Sed would find a way to make it happen. He didn't care what humans or gods thought about it—Mery was the only one who mattered, and if he wanted Sed, he would have him.

Mery supposed this answered his question about whether or not Sed wanted to be with him. It still might only be physical, but at least he knew he wouldn't be rejected.

Sed kissed down Mery's neck, but Mery could feel he was hesitant. He didn't know why, and he never wanted Sed to do anything he didn't want to do. He put his hands on Sed's shoulders and gently pushed until they could look each other in the eyes.

"What?" Sed asked.

"What are we doing?" It might not be the best way to ask, but it was the only way Mery could think of.

"I've been doing it wrong if you don't know what we're doing."

Mery shook his head. "Don't do that. You know what I'm asking, and you don't have to answer if you don't feel up to it, but I don't know if I can do this."

Sed sighed. Thankfully, he didn't let Mery go. Instead, he wrapped his arms around Mery's waist. It was odd to be in this position, sitting in Sed's lap, pressed against him. Mery didn't think he'd ever been in this kind of situation with a man. Every time he'd been with a guy in the past, it had been quick with no time or place for cuddles. Mery hadn't thought he would ever have this, not when he'd been planning on hiding what he was for the rest of his life. It had been necessary to protect his family, and that hadn't changed, even though he was king now.

It was a problem he didn't want to deal with yet. For now,

he wanted to focus on Sed and what was between them. Once he knew, he could freak out about their future.

If they had one.

"You already know I like you," Sed said.

"And I like you. I wouldn't be doing this with you if I didn't. It doesn't tell me what you want, though. Is it just sex? Is it only going to last until you go back to the United States?"

"I already told you I'm not leaving you." Sed's voice was fierce, and Mery believed him, but how long would it last?

Would it only be until he was sure Mery was okay, or could Mery finally allow himself to hope? It was scary, especially considering everything else in his life.

"Because you're keeping me safe. What's going to happen once I am?" It was a question Mery had been asking himself since he and Sed had gotten together after the coronation party. It was a question he still didn't have an answer to, and he was terrified to get one. The fact that he and Sed were having sex didn't mean Sed liked him enough to leave his life behind.

Sed hesitated, and Mery could feel his heart crumble in his chest. It was a painful sensation, and he tried to get to his feet, but Sed refused to let him go. He tightened his hold around Mery's waist and waited until Mery stopped wiggling. Mery gave up. He wasn't strong enough to stay away, not even when he knew it would be best for him.

"I can't make any promises," Sed murmured. "We don't know what's going to happen or how long we have until it does. What I can tell you is . . . that while I wasn't looking forward to spending time here, I changed my mind. I might miss my life in the United States, but it doesn't mean that what I have now isn't good. You're a huge part of that, and I don't want to lose you. But you can't deny things would be complicated if we stayed together in the long term."

Mery sighed and pressed his forehead against Sed's. "I

know things are complicated. You're a god, and I'm the king. I'm supposed to find a nice woman to marry and have children with her, yet here I am, in love with you."

Sed froze for a moment. "You're in love with me?"

Mery hadn't been planning to tell Sed, but he was tired of hiding. He already did enough of that with everyone else. He was hiding that he was gay. He was hiding that he knew the prime minister and Ibuki were planning something. He was hiding that he was in love, and he didn't want to do it anymore, not when it came to Sed. "I am. I don't know when it happened or why, but I can't deny it, and I don't know where that leaves me."

"Where do you *want* it to leave you?"

Mery sighed. Recently, nothing he'd wanted had happened. He was learning to deal with it, and he thought that being the king wouldn't be so bad in the long term, but this had nothing to do with being king. "Ideally? I'd like you to stay, forever if it's at all possible. I want you by my side instead of a woman I don't know. I realize that being with me is probably not something a lot of people want, nor would they want to have to carry the weight of the kingship along with me, but you're probably the best suited person to do it. But of course, you're not a person. You're a god, and you have other things to focus on other than my feelings and what I want."

Sed cupped one of Mery's cheeks. He didn't pull, waiting for Mery to look at him instead of demanding it. When Mery did, he was afraid of what he would see in Sed's gaze. He wasn't quite sure what it was, but he recognized tenderness and maybe love. Or maybe he was fooling himself that Sed wanted the same he did.

"I might be a god, but it doesn't mean I don't love."

"Does that mean that you love me?" Because Mery needed to know. They were talking about their relationship and feelings, but so far, he was the only one who'd said it out loud. If

Sed didn't feel the same way, things would be easy enough. If he did, well, they would become complicated, but it might not be a bad thing. Mery felt that as long as they were together, they could do anything.

"It means I'm in love with you, yes. It means I have no idea what I'm doing. I've always stayed away from relationships with humans."

"But it's not forbidden." Or at least, Mery had never heard about it if it was. He knew that some gods exclusively dated humans. It was all over the papers, and anyone they got with was considered lucky. Besides, he was pretty sure something was happening between Jimmy and Qebui, and no one had said anything about it.

"It's not," Sed confirmed. "But I saw how badly gods treat humans, even the ones they're supposedly in love with. I never wanted to hurt anyone, and I still don't want to hurt you."

"Being with me doesn't have to hurt either of us."

"No, but it'll complicate things. I'm a god, and you're the pharaoh. I don't think things can be more complicated than they already are."

"It doesn't mean we can't be together."

"It doesn't," Sed agreed. "But are you ready to come out to the entire country? The gods won't care that you want to be with me, even though I'm a god and male. What about the prime minister, though? What about your mother?"

"I don't know. I've never thought I would be able to tell my mother or my siblings that I like men. I wasn't planning on ever getting married, and I wouldn't have needed to. Now, most people want me married since I'm the king. I even understand why. It's a heavy weight to carry on your own, and having someone by your side is indispensable. I just don't want that someone to be a person I don't know or trust."

Sed's lips quirked. "So you're not considering the prime

minister's niece?"

"I never considered her. Right now, the only person I want by my side is you. But I realize it's asking a lot. You might be a god, but being with me would make you the king's consort. It's something you have to think about." It was something *Mery* would have to think about, too.

Sed slowly nodded. "How about we both think about it? I know what I want, and I believe you do, too. It doesn't mean we shouldn't consider all the consequences this might have."

"And while we think about it?"

To Mery's relief, Sed kissed him. "Having to think about the future doesn't mean we can't be together. And since you want to be with me for the long term, I think you should come to dinner tonight."

Mery smiled. "Were you planning a romantic dinner for the two of us?"

"No. I'm having dinner with my mother."

Sed could tell Mery was nervous, but the king was doing his best not to show it. Sed was proud, but he knew better than to say it. Mery was working hard, and Sed didn't want to distract him. This wasn't dinner with the prime minister or an important member of the government. It was dinner with Sed's mother, who was a goddess and the mother of the man Mery loved.

Sed was pretty sure he'd be just as nervous if he were to meet Mery's mother. He would find out soon enough, he supposed, but for now, it was best to focus on what was happening tonight rather than what would happen in the future.

Sed knew what he wanted from the future. He would have to sacrifice a lot to get it, but he would also gain so much. He couldn't say he was eager to become the king's consort, and things might not come to that soon, but eventually, he knew they would. If he and Mery stayed in each other's lives, there would be no way out of it. Sed couldn't remain the king's side piece, and he didn't want to.

A knock on the door made both him and Mery stand up straighter. Mery was dressed simply tonight, wearing only a loose pair of pants and a shirt. He looked more modern than usual, but Sed couldn't say he disliked it. Every time he looked at Mery, he wondered how Mery would have looked if he'd been transplanted in Sed's old life. Maybe out of place, but maybe not.

"That will be my mother," he said, moving toward the door.

"Unless you're expecting someone else, I suppose it is," Mery murmured.

Maybe Sed should have asked Jimmy to stick around, but he was pretty sure it would have made things even more awkward, which was the last thing they needed. Besides, his mother had sounded excited at the thought of meeting the king. Sed hadn't told her he and Mery were together, but she would no doubt figure it out soon enough. She'd always had a keen eye when it came to relationships — and Sed.

Sed opened the door. His mother was gorgeous, just like always. Tonight, she wore a flowing green dress and heavy gold earrings. Her hair was pulled up, and she walked in as if she owned the place. She made a beeline for Mery, who was hovering on the side of the room looking as if he didn't know what to do.

"Your highness. It's a pleasure to meet you," Sed's mother said. She took one of Mery's hands in both of hers and squeezed.

Mery looked surprised, but he smiled. "Please, call me Mery. And it's a pleasure to meet you." He hesitated. "I'm not sure what to call you."

Sed's mother laughed. "We're between friends. Please, call

me Satet." She turned to Sed. "I have to say I was surprised you invited me for dinner. Are we celebrating something special?"

Sed had to press his lips together so he wouldn't smile. She'd already seen it, hadn't she?

Sed strode toward them after closing the door and wrapped an arm around Mery's shoulders. He felt Mery tense, but he didn't pull away, for which Sed was grateful. "We're not celebrating anything, but we thought it would be best if Mery met you officially, since we're together."

His mother's eyes glittered. "I have to say you make a handsome couple."

"You don't mind?" Mery blurted out.

"Why would I? Sed being with you means he's going to stay, which is all I ever wanted. I also like you, Mery. You'll be a great king, especially with my son's support and help."

Sed laughed nervously. "I'm not trying to put myself on his throne, Mother."

"Of course not. But you're together, and he's the king. You can't ignore the fact that you'll be involved, no matter how much you might want to."

Sed knew it was pointless to push. Besides, his mother wasn't wrong. If he wanted to be with Mery—and he did, very much so—Sed couldn't ignore the fact that he would eventually be the king's consort.

"Why don't we sit down to eat?" Mery asked, breaking the tension.

Sed could have kissed him, and since he could, he did. He pressed his lips against Mery's temple, smiling when he felt Mery relax against him. His mother was already moving toward the table, and she didn't even look at them, no doubt intentionally giving them privacy. Sed was grateful, and he took the opportunity to kiss Mery on the lips. "Thank you," he murmured.

"I haven't done anything," Mery protested.

"You've done a lot. You're treating my mother as if she were just that. You're not in awe because she's a goddess or anything like that, and this is all I wanted."

"Well, you're a god, too, and it's easy to ignore. I'm trying to look at the two of you as if you were humans, and it's getting easier, especially when she acts as if all this were normal."

Sed's mother was already seated at the table, and Mery and Sed joined her. They were only seated for a moment before the servants came in. Their presence made Sed uncomfortable, but there was no way around it. He'd tried asking if he could cook dinner tonight, and he'd been met with scandalized expressions and apologies that he couldn't. He and Mery might try to find a way around it in the future, but they would have to accept the servants' help for now. Mery had told Sed he'd given everyone who worked at the palace a raise, almost doubling the money they earned, and it made Sed feel less like an asshole. Working at the palace was a sought-out job everyone wanted.

"I suppose you'll be living here rather than at the celestial palace," Sed's mother said.

Sed groaned. "Can we not talk about where I'll be living?"

"I just want to know where my son is. Is that too much to ask?" She looked at Mery as she spoke.

Mery's expression told Sed he didn't want to answer, but he couldn't exactly avoid it. "It would make more sense for him to be staying with me than not," he said slowly.

Sed's mother nodded. "I can't say I ever expected one of my sons to be on the throne, but Sed is the best for that. You chose well, Mery."

Thankfully, the servants came in with the first course, and once they were done serving it, Sed moved the topic of the conversation to something else. The rest of the dinner was more relaxed than Sed had expected. Mery and his mother got along well, and Sed started to feel better. He'd been avoiding his mother for so long that he barely remembered how nice she could be. He'd always focused on how nosy and pushy she was, but there was so much more to her.

He had more proof of that when Ibuki barged in, barely waiting a moment after he'd knocked to open the door. "Your majesty. I've been looking for you everywhere. Thank the gods that one of the servants was able to tell me you were here."

He froze when he saw who Mery was sitting at the table with. His gaze lingered on Sed only for a moment before stopping on Sed's mother.

She looked terrifying. Her eyes were blazing, and now more than ever, Sed could easily believe she'd protected the country's border. Thankfully for Ibuki, she didn't have her bow and arrows with her. It probably didn't fit with the dress.

"Who are you?" she snapped.

Ibuki eyed the door as if he were going to run away. "I apologize. I'm the king's personal assistant."

"And that gives you the right to talk to him that way?"

"Of course not, but it's an emergency."

"What emergency?"

Ibuki clearly hadn't expected her to ask. "Well, it's for the king's ears only."

Sed's mother rose to her feet. "Do you know who I am, Ibuki?"

"A goddess."

"Exactly. If I want to find out what the problem is, I will. Now, is it really an emergency, or did you just want to stick your nose into a situation that's none of your business?"

Ibuki squeaked and reached for the door. "I apologize. I'm sure it can wait until tomorrow, your majesty."

Mery looked like he was about to start laughing. He didn't,

instead gesturing at the door. "I'll see you tomorrow."

Sed's mother sat with a huff as soon as the door was closed behind him. "I can't believe that man. Mery, why haven't you fired him yet? He's so disrespectful."

Mery sighed. "It's not that I don't want to, but who would I replace him with? If I have to choose a new personal assistant, I want someone I can trust with my life."

"How about Sed?"

For a moment, Sed thought he'd heard that wrong. Both Mery and his mother were staring at him, though.

Sed shook his head. "It's not possible. I'm a god. I can't be a personal assistant, not even to the king." Maybe especially not to him, considering their relationship.

"I don't see why not," his mother said. "He trusts you more than anyone else but his family. We both know you would do a better job than that short man who just came in. Besides, that way, you'd be able to keep an eye on Mery. I might not spend a lot of time in the human world, but even I know Mery isn't safe right now."

"I'll think about it," was all Sed could say. He truly would. His mother wasn't wrong when she said it would help keep an eye on Mery.

But could Sed really do it? It felt like the first step toward becoming Mery's consort, which was probably why Sed was hesitant. Everything was moving fast, maybe too fast.

But it felt right, almost as if it was Sed's destiny, and it was inescapable.

CHAPTER SEVEN

"I feel I haven't seen you in a while," Jimmy said a few mornings later as he and Sed sat at the breakfast table.

For some reason, Qebui was there, too. Sed couldn't say he was angry to see his cousin, but he wondered if something was going on between him and Jimmy. He wanted to ask, but he didn't. If Jimmy wanted him to know, he would tell him.

"Things have been busy," Sed said.

"I heard you're to be the king's new personal assistant," Qebui said as he speared a piece of watermelon with his fork.

Sed had been taking a sip of coffee, and he almost spat it in his cousin's face. "How do you know that?"

"I have ears and eyes. Besides, Mery's personal assistant is inefficient. Mery could do worse than firing him for you."

Sed wasn't sure if it was a compliment, so he ignored it. "My mother suggested I could take Ibuki's place. Both she and Mery seem to think it's a great idea."

"It's not?" Jimmy asked. He slipped a piece of bread to Loki, who was sitting at his feet.

The sight made Sed's chest squeeze. He hadn't been spending nearly enough time with his dog and his best friend. Loki was closer than ever to Jimmy, and Sed wondered if the two of them would go back to Pittsburgh soon. That was something else they had to talk about.

"I'm a god, and I'm in a relationship with Mery," Sed explained.

Jimmy looked smug, and Sed was pretty sure he kicked Qebui under the table. Qebui, on the other hand, was gaping at Sed.

"You're really in a relationship with the king?" he asked.

Sed sighed. "I suppose I am, although, to me, he's just Mery."

"But you can't ignore he's the king. People are going to be pissed when they find out, although the fact that you're a god might help smooth things out. Still, you can't give Mery children. That's going to be a problem, especially if things are serious between the two of you."

Sed took another sip of coffee as he thought. "Things *are* serious between us."

"Does that mean we're not going back to Pittsburgh?" Jimmy asked.

Sed looked at him. "I'm not, but it doesn't mean you have to stay."

But Sed wanted him to.

His entire life was changing, and he didn't want to lose his best friend. He would never force Jimmy to stay here, though. Even if Jimmy decided to head back, they could see each other as often as they wanted since Sed was a god. But they hadn't been seeing each other more than a few minutes a day, and they lived in the same palace. What would happen if Jimmy lived on another continent?

"You're leaving?" Qebui asked Jimmy. He sounded oddly vulnerable and hurt—something Sed wasn't used to seeing in him.

Jimmy shook his head. "Not as long as I'm allowed to stay. I don't have anything to go back to, since I lost my job the day before Sed and I moved here."

"What about your family?"

Jimmy grimaced. His family had always been a sore spot for him, and that hadn't changed just because he'd moved away from them. "I'm sure they'll be fine without me. It's not like they'll worry or anything like that. Besides, I like living here. But I should probably find a job if I'm going to stick around."

"You can be Mery's personal assistant," Sed blurted out.

Both Jimmy and Qebui stared. "What?" Jimmy asked.

Sed had never considered it before, but now that he'd thought about it, he couldn't ignore it. "It's the perfect solution. I can't be Mery's PA because I'm a god and his boyfriend." And his consort one day in the future. "People would call it favoritism, and they wouldn't be wrong."

"Being with you isn't why Mery wants you as his PA," Qebui pointed out. "He doesn't trust many people, and I understand why."

"Besides, I'm your best friend," Jimmy added. "Most people would still consider it favoritism."

"But you're human. You might not be from here, but people will be more comfortable dealing with you than with me. At the same time, Mery trusts you, and I do, too. You also need a job, so it's perfect."

Jimmy was still hesitant. "I wouldn't know where to start. I've never been PA to a king, least of all in a country I barely know."

"I'll help you," Qebui offered.

Sed sighed. Those two had been joined at the hip lately, so he wasn't surprised his cousin wanted to help.

"Mery might not even want me as his PA," Jimmy added.

Sed doubted that would be a problem, but for Jimmy, it was. "How about I ask him? If he agrees, the two of you can talk and see if you think you might be a good fit. If you're not, for whatever reason, we'll find someone else, but Mery can't keep Ibuki on for much longer." Not only was he rude and disrespectful, but he was also plotting with the prime minister. He was one of the people Mery should be able to trust with his life, but Sed wouldn't even trust him with Loki's.

Jimmy straightened. "I'll talk to him," he agreed. "I didn't realize things had gotten this bad." He grimaced. "I've been a bad best friend recently, haven't I?"

"We both have been. I've been focused on Mery and everything else, and you've been . . ." Sed wasn't sure how to end that sentence.

"Spending time with me exploring the palace," Qebui finished it for him.

He sounded smug, and when Sed looked at Jimmy, his cheeks were flushed. Sed was going to have to make time for Jimmy and see if he could get him to explain what was going on. He was going to have to make time for Jimmy regardless. Now that things were settling down, he would have the possibility to do that.

He was still worried for Mery and what might happen to him, but he realized he couldn't obsess over that. It wouldn't help, and it would make everyone's life harder. There was no way to know when the prime minister and his allies would act, but from what Sed knew, it was going to take a while. The prime minister wanted Mery to marry his niece and get her pregnant, which wouldn't happen anytime soon—or ever. He might try something else once he realized that, but for now, Mery had agreed to keep Ouser as happy as possible without promising anything, but also without being too clear on what he would and wouldn't do.

It wasn't perfect, and Sed suspected he wouldn't feel better until he knew for sure that Mery's life wasn't in danger anymore, but for now, he was doing everything he could. Taking Ibuki out of the equation would help, and it was a relief to know it would happen soon. If Jimmy didn't think he could be a good PA or if he and Mery weren't a good fit, Sed would have to do it. He didn't want to, but if Jimmy said no, it was the best alternative.

"She'd be excited to spend time with you," Ouser said.

Mery resisted the urge to tell him *he* wouldn't be. The prime minister was yet again talking about his niece, and Mery had enough. He was never going to marry that woman. He didn't even want to talk to her. He felt a bit guilty about it, since he didn't know if she was involved in the whole marriage plot, but he couldn't even stand to hear her name anymore.

He murmured something so the prime minister wouldn't get offended, but he doubted Ouser had even noticed he wasn't eager to meet Aneksi.

"I can arrange your first date, although, of course, I would never assume to know what you like," the prime minister continued. "And I realize an autumn wedding is probably too soon, but maybe spring? Before the weather turns too hot."

Mery slammed his hand on top of his desk before he could stop himself.

It startled the prime minister into closing his mouth, and he stared at Mery with wide eyes.

Mery could probably have found a way to explain his reaction, but he didn't want to. He wanted to tell the truth and for the prime minister to stop talking about his niece.

"Your majesty?" Ouser asked when Mery didn't say anything.

"I apologize for my reaction," Mery started. He was trying to find the best way to tell the prime minister that he was in love with a man, but he doubted there was one. Ouser would freak out, whatever way he said it.

"I'm sorry if I said something to offend you. You and Aneksi can get married whenever you want. I'm sure you don't want to wait too long."

Mery took a deep breath, then another. "Aneksi and I won't be getting married. I've only talked to her once, and while I'm sure she's a very nice woman, she has no appeal to me."

The prime minister paled. "Maybe if you got to know her. I assure you, she's the best woman you could find. She knows her place, and she is strong. She'll bear you many children."

Mery hated having this conversation again. "If I ever have children, I will be adopting them. And, once again, I won't be marrying your niece. I'm already in love with a person, and if they agree to marry me eventually, they're who I want by my side."

"You're in love, your majesty?"

"I am." Mery could leave it at that, but he suspected it wouldn't be enough to stop the prime minister.

He would do everything he could to find out who Mery was spending time with, and there weren't many people on that list. Mery might as well tell him. He and Sed hadn't talked about it, but they both knew that eventually, they would have to come out to the world. Right now felt perfect to Mery, or at least, as good as any other moment might be.

Mery cleared his throat. "I'm sure you're aware that I've been spending a lot of time with Sed."

The prime minister blinked. "The god?"

"The god," Mery confirmed. "As we spent time together, we fell in love."

The prime minister's jaw dropped. "But he's a man."

"I'm very much aware of that. It's one of the reasons I can't marry your niece. I've never been interested in women, and that's not going to change."

Ouser shot to his feet on the other side of Mery's desk. "You can't be serious. You're the king. You *have* to marry a woman, and no one can find out you were ever interested in men."

"You can't force me to marry anyone."

"There are laws—"

"And I can change them. Don't force my hand, Ouser. I

107

might not know what I'm doing yet, but I will eventually, and if you continue to behave the way you've been behaving, you might not be my prime minister by then. I don't appreciate being pushed in a direction I don't want to go or to be told I'm breaking the law."

Mery wasn't sure there was a law against same-sex relationships. It was something he normally would have asked his PA to look into, but there was no way he was asking Ibuki. Besides, even if there was such a law, Sed was a god. No one would dare say anything against his and Mery's relationship. And if there *was* such a law, Mery would change it. Who he loved and who he was with didn't change who he was, and the same went for everyone else.

"Your majesty, this is impossible. You can't be in a relationship with a god, and you certainly can't marry one. He's playing with you. It's what gods do."

Mery could stand listening to the prime minister telling him he was breaking the law, but he wasn't going to sit there while the man insulted Sed. He got to his feet, too, and Ouser took a step back. It was almost as if he expected Mery to hit him, which Mery found hilarious.

"The meeting is over," Mery told him.

"But we haven't discussed—"

"And we won't, not today. I expect you to be more respectful the next time we see each other."

Mery didn't give the prime minister time to answer. He turned around and left through the open garden door, never once looking back. He breathed more easily once he was outside, but he was still overwhelmed and angry. He didn't even notice he was walking toward Sed's rooms until he got there. He looked down the wall at the door that led to his own suite, but he decided against it. He didn't want to be alone right now.

He raised his hand and knocked on the doorframe, since

the door was open. It took a moment for Sed to answer, and when he did, he smiled until he noticed Mery's expression. "What happened?" he asked as he ushered Mery inside.

Mery froze when he saw that Qebui and Jimmy were sitting at the table. There was still food on it, as if the three of them had been having breakfast recently.

"I'm sorry to interrupt you," Mery said.

"You're not interrupting anything. What happened?"

When Mery didn't move, Sed put a hand on the small of his back and gently pushed him toward the table.

There was a fourth chair, and Mery sat in it while Sed settled back into his seat. He had to tell Sed what had just happened so he would know their relationship wasn't a secret anymore, but he didn't know if Sed had told his friends yet. Even if he hadn't, they would no doubt find out soon enough.

"I had a meeting with the prime minister," Mery started.

"I know. Did it go badly?"

"That's an understatement," Mery said with a chuckle. He had to laugh if he didn't want to cry. "I might have ruined everything."

Sed reached over the table and took one of Mery's hands. "I'm sure that whatever happened, it's not as bad as you think."

"He was talking about my wedding to his niece. He was already choosing a date, and I snapped. I told him I'd never marry her and that I would never marry any woman because I was in love with a man."

Sed winced. "Okay, so maybe it *was* a disaster."

"I told him who I was in love with. I'm not sure what scandalized him more—that you're a god or that you're a man. He even said that us being together was against the law, but I don't know if he was lying."

"We'll have to look into it."

Mery rubbed his face. "I would ask Ibuki to do it, but I can't trust him."

"I'll do it," Jimmy said.

Mery looked at him. "You'll do what?"

"Sed asked me to be your personal assistant. He thinks it would be a better idea than him doing it, and I agree. I can't promise I'll do a good job, though. I've done this kind of work before, but never for a king, and I'm new in this country. It'll probably be a disaster."

Mery found himself laughing. "Even if it is, it can't be worse than what's already happening."

But his secrets were out. Now, he and Sed could be open about being together, even though it would be hard. There were many more hurdles in front of them, but at least Mery wouldn't face them alone.

They were exposed. Sed had known it would happen eventually, probably sooner than either of them would have been ready for, but he hadn't thought it would be this soon. They had to do some damage control, but he wasn't sure either of them was in the right state of mind to do that.

To his surprise, Qebui got to his feet. "I think that the first thing to do is fire Ibuki and replace him with Jimmy, make it official. That way, Jimmy will be able to protect Mery from people who want to talk to him and he doesn't want to see. I doubt the prime minister will keep this to himself, which means a lot of people will want a royal meeting."

Mery groaned. "I should have kept my mouth shut."

"Maybe you didn't do this the best or even the right way, but no one should be allowed to shame you into marrying someone. You shouldn't be ashamed of yourself for who you love."

Sed hadn't been sure what to think of Qebui recently, but his words reminded him why he'd been so close to his cousin once. Now that he was planning on staying, he had every intention of fixing the relationship between them. It would have to wait, unfortunately.

"I'm not ashamed," Mery said. "But I made a mess."

"But you stood up for yourself," Sed intervened.

They'd been working on Mery standing up for himself for a while, but it was always hard for him. He felt like he didn't know what he was talking about, and in most situations, he didn't. He'd only been crowned king a few weeks ago, and while he'd been working his ass off to catch up with everything he needed to know, it would take a while. The fact that Ibuki and the prime minister had been throwing wrenches in his plans hadn't helped, either.

Hopefully, that would change now. With Ibuki out of the way, the prime minister was the last person plotting against Mery, at least that Sed knew of. There was no doubt in his mind that other people weren't happy at having him on the throne, but Sed wasn't as worried about them as he was about the prime minister.

"What about the prime minister?" Mery asked.

"He'll be harder to remove," Sed said slowly. "It should be possible, though. I suggest you talk to the other ministers. I'm sure some will be on the prime minister's side, but not all of them. Some will take this opportunity to get rid of him, but others will agree with you. No one is universally loved, especially not him."

But it would take time, and in the meantime, the prime minister would be allowed to do what he wanted. Sed suspected that the man already knew Mery would try to remove him, which meant he would strike before that could happen. If he lost his job as prime minister, he would lose everything he'd been working toward to. He wouldn't allow that to happen, which meant Mery was in danger.

Sed was going to have to stay with him even more often

than he already was. It was the only way to keep him safe, but Sed still had work to do. He'd been looking into the guards in case some were related to the prime minister. He hadn't been surprised to find out that was the case. He needed Mery's approval to fire them, or at the very least, to move them to other areas. They couldn't afford to have anyone who was friendly with the prime minister protecting the king.

All of this would be easier to do once Ibuki wasn't Mery's personal assistant anymore. That was the most urgent thing to do, and even though Jimmy wasn't sure it was the best idea, Sed had faith in him.

Together, they would make this work. They had to.

Qebui left the room. He'd said he was going to find Ibuki, and Sed trusted he would fire the man. Qebui was probably the best person for the job, or maybe the second-best behind Sed's mother. She wasn't here now, and Sed was more than happy to let Qebui deal with it.

"What now?" Mery asked. He sounded and looked exhausted, even though it was barely ten in the morning.

"Why don't you take the day off?" Jimmy suggested.

"I'm the king. I can't take a day off."

"Why not? You're exhausted, and as far as I'm aware, you've been working for weeks without time off. No one can go on like that forever, not even you. Besides, it's going to take me at least a few hours, probably more, to go over Ibuki's paperwork. That should give you time to sleep, or at least to stop thinking about your job for a while."

Mery stared at Jimmy. "I think I'm going to like working with you."

Jimmy's cheeks turned pink. "I hope I won't disappoint you."

"As long as you don't stab me in the back or plot to put someone else on the throne, I don't think you will. It feels good to be able to trust the person who will be working the most closely with me."

Sed agreed. Ibuki would still be a worry, if anything because he knew everything there was to know about the palace while Jimmy didn't. It would take a while for people to accept him and treat him like they had Ibuki, and in the meantime, things would be dicey. Sed wasn't one to give up easily, though. He was doing this for Mery, and Mery was doing it for the country.

It would have been easy for him to allow Ibuki and the prime minister to take charge and do whatever they wanted, but he'd stood up for himself. He might never have wanted to be king, but he was doing everything he could to be a good one. The fact that the prime minister had been limiting him instead of helping him hadn't helped, but that would be over soon.

Sed was relieved he wouldn't have to be Mery's personal assistant. It was too soon for him to become king consort, but he didn't fool himself into thinking he could wait forever. Mery needed him, and he had no problem stepping up.

He'd never imagined this when he'd left Pittsburgh. He'd thought it would be for a few weeks, yet here he was, planning his future with Mery. The fact that Jimmy wasn't going anywhere helped, but realizing that Sed's home was where the people he loved were had helped even more so.

This was where Mery was, and Sed couldn't leave. He didn't even want to anymore. He had no idea how big the problems they were going to have to deal with were, but he was ready to face all of them. Staying and becoming king consort was a sacrifice he was willing to make to be with Mery.

Having Mery in his life was enough for Sed to forget his dreams, or rather, to change them.

CHAPTER EIGHT

Mery was warm and safe, and he didn't want to get up and face the day. He wanted to stay in bed with Sed and take another day off, but yesterday had been enough. He had to find out what was going on, and he hoped Jimmy had managed to do some damage control.

He hadn't heard from the prime minister since he'd left his office yesterday morning. He didn't *want* to hear from him, but he was the king. He couldn't ignore what had happened or what he'd done.

He looked to the side. Sed was next to him, still asleep, and Mery decided he would sneak out of bed without waking him. It wasn't his problem, and he shouldn't have to deal with it. He'd already done so much for Mery, and this felt like too much to ask.

When Mery slid to the side to fling his legs off the bed, an arm hooked around his waist and pulled him back.

Mery fit perfectly against Sed's chest. He sighed and allowed Sed to hold him, at least for a moment. He couldn't stay, unfortunately. "I have to go to work," he murmured.

Sed kissed the back of Mery's neck. "It can wait five minutes."

"I think it's already later than it ought to be."

"If *you* can't be late, I don't know who can."

That much was true. No one would dare say anything about Mery's lateness, but it wouldn't feel right anyway.

Mery had never expected that being king would be easy, but he still felt he was working against people who should be

114

helping him. Hopefully, now that Ibuki was out of the picture, things would become easier. There was still the prime minister to deal with, as well as the other ministers. Who knew what the prime minister had told them?

Mery supposed he would find out soon enough.

But first he allowed Sed to pull him closer. No matter what happened out there, what the day held, Mery knew he would come back to Sed this evening, and that was enough to give him strength. He suspected he would need a lot of it, but for once, he wasn't alone. If he needed anything, he could ask Sed, Jimmy, or Qebui. He'd never had this many people by his side, and he knew it would help.

And if it didn't, well, he was the king. He would deal with whatever was thrown at him, whether he wanted to or not.

"Have you heard from Jimmy?" Sed asked.

"Not since yesterday morning. He told me to take the day off, and he stayed away."

"Good. You needed time off."

"I feel guilty." Mery wasn't surprised. Ever since Ibuki had found him when he'd still been a farmer, it had been hammered into him that he had responsibilities he couldn't shirk. The problem was that once he'd arrived at the palace, Ibuki and the prime minister had done everything they could to make sure he *didn't* shoulder them. Mery hadn't even realized how contradicting the two men had been until recently, and he blamed himself for that, too.

Hopefully, it was in the past. Mery would need to find a new prime minister, and he couldn't think of anyone. He was tempted to ask a god, but there was no way Sed would agree to that, and he didn't think Qebui would, either. Besides, the ministers and the people who lived in the country would no doubt have something to say about that. Maybe not openly, since it would be a god, but Mery knew enough to realize it was a bad idea.

The problem was that he didn't trust anyone else. He wanted to, but so far, no one had shown him they were trustworthy.

Sed sighed. "I understand why you feel that way, but you shouldn't. I've been around a long time, Mery. I've dealt with dozens of different kings, and I've seen the way they worked. It's important to take time for yourself, especially because you won't have many occasions to do that. Everyone needs time off, even the king, maybe especially him. It'll be one crisis after another, and having a day to breathe between them will be the only way for you to go on."

"But yesterday probably wasn't the best day to take it. I should have dealt with Ibuki myself. It wasn't right to ask Qebui to do it."

Sed smiled against Mery's neck. "Maybe not, but he didn't have a problem doing it. He'd been looking forward to it since he met Ibuki."

"Who chose him, do you think?" It was a question Mery had never asked. He hadn't even thought about it. Ibuki had knocked on his door and had told him who he was and what he was expected to do. But who had put him in charge?

"The prime minister," Sed answered. "I suspect they were already planning something when they first talked to you."

"How could they have?"

"Well, the prime minister knew he would have to step back and allow you to make the decisions he'd been making until recently. We both know he doesn't like it, and it would make sense for him to try to influence you or do something before you were even at court."

"That means he's not going to like it when he finds out Ibuki doesn't work for me anymore."

"He already knows."

Mery frowned and sat up so he could look down at Sed. "How do you figure?"

Sed followed Mery's example and sat. The sheets pooled around his waist, and it took Mery a second to be able to tear his gaze away from Sed's chest and look him in the eyes.

Sed seemed amused, and he reached out to kiss Mery's cheek. "You really think Ibuki wouldn't tell him? It was the first thing he did once Qebui fired him. The prime minister tried to reach you yesterday, but we made sure he couldn't."

Mery winced. "He's going to be angry."

"Who cares? He's not the king—*you* are. You decided to fire your personal assistant, and the prime minister has nothing to do with that decision. If he asks for an explanation, tell him exactly that."

"I never wanted to make an enemy out of him."

"And you didn't. He did that himself, and once all of this is over and he doesn't work for you anymore, he will still be responsible for it. I realize it's easy for you to feel responsible for a lot of things since you're in charge, but you can't think like that."

Mery rubbed his face. He needed to get up and shower to start his day, but this conversation felt important. "How can I not feel responsible? I'm the king."

Sed put a hand on Mery's shoulder. "And you already have than enough decisions to make. You can't force people to do what you want or think is right, though. You're not a dictator. Everyone in the country has free will, which includes choosing whether or not they want to follow the rules and laws. The only thing *you* can do is make sure those rules are as fair as possible."

Mery leaned against Sed's chest. He had no idea what today held for him, and he wasn't looking forward to it, but knowing he wouldn't be alone anymore helped. If he needed anything, Sed would be there for him. Mery would have to try not to rely on him too much, especially since while things had become official between them, Sed wasn't his consort yet.

They hadn't talked about it, but they would have to. Mery was afraid to rock the boat, even though he kept telling himself he shouldn't be.

Sed had made his decision. He was staying with Mery, and he knew everything that entailed. But he was a god, and Mery couldn't help but wonder if he would be enough. He felt like he didn't have a lot to offer, and most days, he didn't understand what Sed saw in him. He also didn't understand why anyone had wanted him to be king.

But he *was* king, and he was with Sed. There was no way out of the first, and he didn't want a way out of the second.

Sed wished he and Mery had been able to stay in bed the rest of the morning, but unfortunately, they both had things to do. Mery had a lot of responsibilities. And while Sed had promised he would keep an eye on him, the few times he had, he'd found him and Jimmy working together as if they'd done it all their lives. Thankfully, Qebui hadn't been far, and he'd done his best to keep everyone away from the office. Since he was a god, he was successful, but Sed didn't fool himself into thinking it would last forever.

That was why he was walking along the palace's hallways. Even with Ibuki out of the equation, Mery was still in danger. That meant Sed had to find out what was going on, and soon. Mery might be able to start doing his job now, but the prime minister wasn't going to stay away and watch him do it. He would do something, and Sed wanted to be ready when it happened.

More than the prime minister, he was worried about Anhur. He was a god, which meant it would be harder to deal with him than with the prime minister. Sed couldn't just threaten him. He would have to involve someone higher than both of them in the godly hierarchy, which he wasn't looking forward to. Even if he managed, he didn't know what the other gods would think. They seldom cared what happened to humans, and even though they'd been the one to choose Mery as the king and their messenger, Sed had a hard time imagining any of them caring about what happened to him. If Mery died, they would replace him, and that was that.

Sed and Qebui were the only ones for whom Mery mattered, along with maybe a few other gods. Sed wished he could contact Nu, since there was no one higher up than them, but he also didn't want to bother them for something like this. They'd seemed happy with Mery after the coronation ceremony, but it didn't mean they would want to be involved in whatever was going on.

Sed turned a corner and almost collided with someone. He reached out to grab them, smiling when he saw who was standing in front of him. "Iah?"

The moon god blinked at Sed. "Sed?"

Sed grinned. He and Iah had been great friends once. Sed should have reached out to him when he'd come back, but he'd been so busy that he hadn't found the time. "What are you doing here?"

Iah took a step back. "I heard you were back, but I didn't believe it. I didn't believe you wouldn't come to see me if you were."

Sed's chest felt tight. "I should have. It's been a mess. Do you know anything about what's going on?"

Iah hesitated. "I've been told you and the king are together."

Sed looked around. The hallway was empty except for them, so he felt safe enough to explain what was going on. "I am. That's not the reason I didn't come see you, though." It was one of them, but not the main one. "Someone is plotting against him. There are gods involved, and I can't leave him until I know he's safe."

Iah crossed his arms over his chest. "Isn't that the case with all the kings? There's always someone who wants to knock them off the throne. Did you really think your king would be different?"

Iah's tone wasn't harsh, but this wasn't like him. He was angry, and while Sed understood and felt sorry, his priority was still Mery and his safety. "I'm not surprised people want him off the throne. Normally, I'd stay away, but I'm with him. I can't ignore what's going on, and I can't focus on anything or anyone else until I'm sure he's as safe as possible."

"Not even on your oldest friends?"

Sed rubbed his face. "I know I was wrong. I should have come to see you and Qebui and everyone else as soon as I arrived. I shouldn't have left the way I did in the first place. I'll always regret the way I acted, but I can't change it."

"No one is asking you to change it. We're just asking you to care about us."

"And I do. But I care about Mery, too, and he's human. He's more vulnerable, and I don't know what I would do if something happened to him."

Iah stared at Sed for a moment.

Sed wondered what he was going to say. He'd always liked Iah, who usually was a gentle, understanding god. Sed had behaved badly with him and with a lot of other people, though, and he wouldn't blame him for not wanting to see him. But Iah was here. It had to mean something. He could be here to see Qebui, but Sed had never known them to be friends.

Iah eventually sighed. His shoulders relaxed, and while he still looked wary, Sed thought he wasn't angry anymore. "Who's involved? You mentioned a god."

"I'm sure of Anhur. He came to talk to me and try to convince me to go home."

"But you didn't because you love Mery."

120

"And because I realized that my home was where the people I loved are, not in an apartment away from everyone."

Iah rolled his eyes. "The king truly has to be a special man to get you to talk that way."

"He is. He never wanted to be king, but he did what he thought was right for his family and for the country. I admire him for that, and I don't want him to be hurt because of it. It would have been easier for him to say no and keep on living his old life. It's not fair for us to thank him by leaving him alone when he's in danger."

Iah raised his hands. "You don't have to convince me. Unfortunately, I doubt there's a lot I can do for you. You should talk to one of the big five."

Sed swallowed. He'd been afraid of that, and he wasn't looking forward to it. That was possibly worse than talking to Nu themself. "I don't think any of them will want to listen to me."

"Probably not. It's not going to be easy, but they're your best bet to put an end to it. Anhur will have to listen to them and obey whatever order they give him."

"If they give one. I doubt they care much about Mery's safety."

"Maybe not, but someone gave the order to find a new king. That someone will care. Find out who it was and talk to them."

Sed grimaced. "Qebui thinks it was Ra."

Iah stared at him for a moment as if he expected him to confess it was a joke. The problem was that it wasn't.

"That's going to complicate things. It doesn't mean it's impossible, though. If you truly want to protect your king, you'll find a way."

They both jumped when someone started screaming down the hallway. They looked at each other, then, as if they'd decided together, they turned toward the sound and started running.

Sed had no way to know what happened, but it didn't sound good. Hopefully, it was just a servant, but he could feel in his heart that something had happened to Mery. He didn't know where that certainty came from, and he didn't care. He just wanted to get to Mery.

Guards ran all over the palace. They were all going in the same direction, so Sed followed them. He wasn't surprised to see it led him to Mery's office, and he pushed past people, trying to get to the doors. Two of the people he cared the most for worked there, and they were both human.

A few of the guards tried to pull him away, but a well-placed glare and a bit of electricity sparking from his fingertips were enough to get them to step back. Sed managed to reach the door, where he found Qebui standing.

"What's going on?" he asked.

"Where were you?"

"Trying to find out what was going on. Tell me, Qebui."

Qebui stared at Sed for a second. Then, his expression shifted. "Someone tried to kill him."

Sed's mouth went dry. "To kill who? What *happened*, Qebui?"

"Someone tried to kill Mery."

Mery couldn't look away from the man on the floor. Blood was spreading around him, making Mery's stomach feel like he was about to throw up, but no matter how much he tried not to stare, he couldn't stop.

That man had tried to kill him. He would have succeeded if Jimmy hadn't been there.

Finally, Mery managed to tear his gaze away from the man on the floor. He looked at Jimmy instead, who was standing next to him as if still trying to protect him. "Thank you," Mery said. His voice was rough, but he doubted anyone would ask why.

Jimmy shrugged, then instantly winced. "Don't worry about it. I would have done it for anyone."

That almost made Mery smile. "I'm anyone, then?"

"You're not. You're my best friend's boyfriend. You're my friend. I won't allow anyone to hurt you if there's anything I can do to stop them."

"I already asked the doctors to come."

Jimmy looked at his arm. He was bleeding from a deep cut in his bicep, and while it had to hurt, Mery didn't think it would be deadly. Jimmy had put himself between Mery and the guard, which was the only reason Mery was still alive.

A commotion at the open door made both of them glance toward it. Sed pushed past Qebui, looked around for a second, then made a beeline for Mery. He wrapped his arms around Mery before Mery could say anything, and Mery allowed himself a moment to relax.

He was safe. He'd been safe even before Sed arrived, but now he knew he was for sure, and he felt better.

Sed leaned back but didn't let go of Mery. "What happened?" he asked.

Mery's gaze went back to the guard on the floor. "He tried to stab me."

Sed looked down at the guard, too. The man had slit his throat when he'd realized he'd failed at killing Mery, even though Mery had told him not to do it. He hadn't wanted anyone to die, not even the man who'd tried to kill him. Now, he would never be able to be in his office without thinking about what had just happened.

It wasn't just that. Whatever had happened, whoever had paid this man to kill him, the guard hadn't deserved to die, especially not the way he had.

Sed looked at Mery again. "But you're safe. Are you hurt?"

"I'm fine, but Jimmy stepped between us. He was stabbed."

Sed's eyes widened, and he turned to his best friend. Jimmy waved at him, clearly intending on telling him he was fine. "It burns, but I'll be fine."

"I would kill him myself if he wasn't dead already," Qebui growled.

He hadn't been in the room when the guard had tried to kill Mery, but he'd arrived seconds later, and he'd freaked out over Jimmy being wounded. Mery had often wondered what was going on between the two of them, and while he didn't know for sure, he could tell they cared about each other.

Sed guided Mery toward the closest chair. Mery wanted to tell him he was okay again, but he could understand why Sed wanted to take care of him. If their roles had been reversed, he would be fussing, too.

Mery looked at Jimmy, but Qebui was already taking care of him, pushing him into yet another chair. Jimmy looked like he wanted to protest, but he didn't, and he looked relieved once his ass was on the chair.

"Tell me what happened," Sed asked.

"I'm honestly not sure," Mery told him. "Jimmy and I were working. He was telling me everything he'd managed to do yesterday and what had happened with Ibuki, and we barely heard the door open. When I looked up, a guard was walking in. I thought he was there to tell me something, or maybe to warn me that someone wanted to talk to me. He came closer, and I got to my feet. I didn't even think he might hurt me. I barely saw the knife, but Jimmy did, and he jumped in front of me. Everything went so quickly."

Mery wasn't sure he could continue, and he was relieved when Jimmy did. "The guy stabbed me in the arm, then raised his knife again. Before he could hurt Mery, I punched him like you taught me," he told Sed. "It took a few punches, but he finally went down. By the time he did, more guards were streaming in, trying to stop him. He looked around, then, he used the knife he'd stabbed me with to slit his own throat."

Mery had to force himself not to look at the man again. There were guards around him now, probably wondering what they should do with him. Mery wanted to ask them to take the body away, but he thought there would be an investigation, and whoever would be in charge probably needed the body to stay where it was, at least for a bit. The guards weren't the only ones hovering around the body. There was a man Mery didn't know, but he thought he'd walked in with Sed. He eyed the man, wondering who it was. He didn't have to ask. Sed had probably noticed he was staring, and he took one of Mery's hands and squeezed.

"That's Iah. Once, he, Qebui, and I were inseparable."

"Where did he come from?" Mery asked before he could realize it was probably rude to ask.

Set didn't seem to care. "I don't know. We bumped into each other and started talking. I told him what was happening, and he gave me a suggestion. I'm not looking forward to it, but I think he's right. I'll have to talk to one of the big fives."

Qebui made a strangled sound, but Mery didn't know who Sed was talking about. He could imagine, though. Neither Sed nor Qebui were important gods, but all gods were linked to each other. Sed might not be significant enough to make decisions when it came to other gods, but some could. They were in charge, very much the way Mery was.

"What is going on here?" a loud voice asked from the door.

Mery groaned when the guards parted to allow the prime minister to come in. They didn't even ask, but then, he was the prime minister.

His step faltered when he saw the guard on the floor. Mery stared, trying to read the man's expression. Had he been the one to send the guard to kill him? It would make sense, especially after Ibuki had been fired yesterday. Mery didn't want to believe it, but he couldn't ignore the flash of fury in Ouser's eyes when he looked at Mery again. "What happened?" the prime minister asked.

Sed got to his feet. "I don't think now is the best moment to ask that kind of question," he said. "The king was attacked, and his personal assistant stabbed. It can wait."

Ouser barely glanced at Jimmy. "Where's Ibuki?"

"He was fired yesterday. Jimmy is the king's new personal assistant, and he's the one who saved his life."

Ouser opened his mouth, no doubt to say something rude, but Mery didn't have it in himself to listen. He got to his feet and instantly swayed. Thankfully, Sed was there, already reaching for him. Mery smiled at him and, not looking at the prime minister again, said, "I'd like to go to my rooms."

"I'll take you."

"Your majesty, you can't do that," the prime minister protested.

"What part of *he was attacked* didn't you understand?" Sed snapped. "He needs rest. He just saw a man kill himself after trying to stab him. You can talk to him tomorrow, once he feels better. In the meantime, he'll be in his rooms, and no one is to disturb him." Sed looked around as he spoke. It was obvious to everyone that this was an order.

Sed led Mery toward the door. Qebui and Jimmy weren't far behind, and Mery wasn't surprised to see Iah follow them. He'd never talked to the god, but if he was a friend of Sed, he was a friend of Mery's, too. They were silent as they walked toward Mery's rooms, and Mery tried to keep his back straight and act as if nothing had happened. He could hear the prime minister's raised voice behind them, but he didn't stop.

The silence lasted until they reached Mery's rooms. As soon as they were inside, his limbs started trembling. He was relieved when Sed hugged him close, and he leaned against him, relishing in the thought that he wasn't alone to face this.

"I'll tell the healers we're here," Iah said. He walked out again, closing the door behind himself.

"What are we going to do?" Jimmy asked.

"*You* are going to rest," Qebui told him.

Jimmy glared at him. "Stop that. I'm fine, and you don't need to hover over me as if I'm about to die. Someone tried to stab Mery, though. Things are getting worse, and we were lucky I was there with him when it happened. What if next time I'm not? We have to put an end to this."

"I don't know if the big five will want to step in," Sed said.

"And you won't find out until you ask. Why don't you do that?"

"I will."

Mery couldn't help but wonder what they would do if the big five said no. What could they do if the powerful gods refused to involve themselves in what was happening and allowed Anhur and the prime minister to hurt him?

Sed was so angry he felt he could kill someone. He wanted to go out there, find Anhur, and beat his ass into the ground until Anhur couldn't speak anymore. It was near impossible to kill a god, even a minor one, but Sed was willing to try. Every time he looked at Mery, he realized how close he'd come to losing him, and he felt like he couldn't breathe.

"We could bring in other gods," Qebui said. He sounded hesitant, which wasn't like him.

Sed swallowed a few times until he was ready to speak without sounding angry. "What do you have in mind?"

"If the big five won't intervene, maybe gods from another pantheon could."

Sed stared at him. "What are you talking about?"

Qebui shrugged. "It's worth a try."

"You were offended because my dog's name is Loki."

"I wasn't offended. I thought it was weird, and I still do. Loki would find it hilarious, though."

Sed continued staring. "You know Loki?"

"I know people. You don't have to sound so surprised."

"He's not an Egyptian god."

"So? You made friends. I did the same, and he might come in useful. Loki is more powerful than both of us, and if the big five won't intervene, he might."

"Why would he care? He's a Norse god." And it was too easy to imagine what an uproar it would be if he tried to intervene in this situation.

"Exactly. He would find it funny to stick his nose into this because he knows he shouldn't. He's stronger than most of the gods. Don't tell anyone I said this, but I'm pretty sure he's stronger than the big five."

Sed had never had anything to do with gods from other pantheons. It was enough of a mess for him to have to deal with his family, and he never intended to contact anyone outside of it. He knew about them, though. Everyone did. There were a lot of stories about Loki and how he behaved, so Sed wasn't surprised the man wouldn't hesitate to step into this situation, even though he probably was one of the few. What he *was* surprised at was that Qebui was friends with him.

He wasn't convinced. "I don't know. This is already enough of a mess. I don't think we should make things worse by asking another god to intervene. Maybe we should keep that as a last resort."

Qebui grimaced. "That might be a problem then, because the last time he contacted me, I told him what was happening. He said he'd be coming around."

Sed groaned and buried his face against Mery's shoulder. "This is going to be a disaster, isn't it?"

Mery patted Sed's arm. "Maybe not. His presence might be enough for the prime minister to realize I have more allies than he thinks."

Sed hoped that was all they needed, but he wasn't an idiot. The prime minister had no doubt organized the attempted assassination, and the only reason he'd dared do it was that he had backing from the gods. It might only be Anhur, but knowing Anhur, he wouldn't back down in front of anything or anyone. He always thought he was the strongest and scariest, even though nothing could be further from the truth.

But if the big five refused to help, this might be what they had to deal with. Hopefully, it wouldn't come to that, but Sed couldn't deny he was relieved to know that he would have help if it did. "You think you can keep him under control?" he asked, looking at Qebui again.

"I don't think anyone can keep Loki under control. I'll ask him to be calm as a favor to me, though."

A knock on the door made all of them jump. Qebui was on his feet before Sed could react, and his back was ramrod straight when he opened the door. He relaxed when Iah walked in, followed by two doctors who looked like they'd rather be anywhere but here. Sed didn't know why, and right now, he didn't care.

"My personal assistant was wounded," Mery said, getting to his feet. "He was defending me, and I want him to be given the best care."

One of the doctors still looked hesitant, but the other nodded and moved toward Jimmy. "Of course, your majesty. Can I ask what happened?"

"He was stabbed."

The doctor tsked. "You'd think that with all the guards around here, people in the palace would be safer."

The wary doctor sucked in a breath, but Mery didn't seem to care. "It was a guard who attacked us, actually. I don't care how much it costs or how much time you need. Make sure Jimmy is okay."

The doctor glared at him. "We would have done that regardless."

"That's good to hear." He hesitated. "Can I have your names?"

The first doctor was already next to Jimmy, but he looked up at Mery. "I'm Minmes, but you can call me Min."

Mery turned his attention to the other doctor. She was still staring, but she managed to get her name out. "I'm Satiah, your majesty."

Mery nodded. "Thank you. Please, take care of Jimmy."

As they did so, Sed took Mery's hand and pulled him toward the bedroom they now shared. He needed some time alone with him to make sure Mery was okay. Mery seemed amused, but he didn't protest, not even when Sed closed the door behind them. Sed knew Mery wanted to be with Jimmy and make sure he was okay, and he would. First, though, Sed wanted some time alone with the man he loved.

"How are you?" Sed asked. He cupped both of Mery's cheeks and looked him in the eyes.

Mery's body relaxed. "I've been better, but I'm okay, at least physically. It was terrifying, though. I don't know what I would have done if Jimmy hadn't been there."

It was too easy to imagine what would have happened. If Jimmy hadn't been there, Mery might have been killed, and Sed's heart would have been broken. That wasn't even considering what would have happened if the king had died. Sed was thinking only of his personal pain, and right now, he didn't care about anything else.

"I want to confront Anhur," he told Mery.

Mery frowned. "Why? You already know he's involved."

"I'm hoping I can change his mind."

"Do you really think you'll manage? He's in this for

something, and if he's anything like the prime minister, he won't stop until he gets it. Apparently, that's my death."

"I won't allow him or anyone else to hurt you. I'd die first."

Mery snorted. "You're a god. You can't die."

"Which is why I'm never leaving your side again. If someone else tries to hurt you, I'll put myself between the two of you. I don't want you or Jimmy to be hurt again."

"I don't want you to be hurt, either. I don't know if confronting Anhur will help, but I won't stop you if you feel you have to do it. I don't think I could even if I tried."

"It probably won't," Sed admitted. "And I don't want to do something you don't approve of."

"You're going to eventually." Mery kissed Sed. "Just like I'll do things you don't approve of. But we'll talk them through, and we'll find a compromise. In this case, I understand why you want to talk to Anhur, and I won't try to stop you. Something has to be done, and I don't think anything I can do will be enough. I could arrest the prime minister, but I don't have any proof he's involved, which gives him the opportunity to try again. If I tried to arrest him, he would use that against me. The last thing we want is for him to take my place on the throne."

"He doesn't have a right to it as things are."

"No, but he was in charge before I arrived. If anything happens to me, people will want to go back to how things were before, and I don't blame them. Most days, I want that, too. But there's no going back, and I'll do everything I can to keep the country safe, even from the prime minister."

The task that awaited them wouldn't be an easy one, but Sed thought that together, they could do this. They had to, because he didn't want to think about what the alternative would be.

CHAPTER NINE

Sed wanted to punch someone, preferably Anhur or one of the big five. None of them had agreed to talk to him, let alone intervene and stop what was happening. Apparently they hadn't been the ones to want a king on the throne, so they didn't care what happened to Mery. Sed had tried to go even higher, but he hadn't even been allowed in the same wing of the celestial palace as Ra. He wouldn't be able to get to him, and he didn't know who else to ask.

He couldn't prove Anhur was behind everything. Anhur were hiding in the celestial palace, and Sed couldn't waste time visiting the place often.

He'd promised Mery he would stay with him as much as he could, and he'd kept that promise. Every morning, he and Mery had breakfast together. Once that was done, they headed to Mery's office and worked there until lunch. They had lunch together, then worked during the afternoon, had dinner, and went to bed. They did all of that together, which meant Sed hadn't been able to investigate as much as he wanted to.

Mery's family had visited him after he'd almost been stabbed. They'd been frantic and wary, and after Mery had introduced Sed as his consort, shocked. Sed didn't know if they would accept it, and it was one more thing that tore Mery apart, but neither of them could focus on that for now.

Qebui had taken over Sed's investigation into Anhur. Sed wouldn't have trusted him a few months ago, but now, he did. Qebui was as angry at him for what had happened.

Jimmy was healing, and he kept saying he was fine, but Sed knew he had nightmares. Mery did, too, and every time Sed thought about it, he wanted to hit someone even more.

They were doing everything they could, but the prime minister was still in his place, and he smiled smugly every time Sed saw him. He thought nothing could be done to stop him, and he might be right. If Sed and Qebui couldn't get a more powerful god to help, it would be near impossible to remove the prime minister. They hadn't been able to find any kind of proof that he was involved, and Sed suspected they wouldn't, no matter how hard they dug.

The prime minister might be in trouble if they managed to get Anhur out of the equation, or he might not. It was something they had to do either way, and Sed was racking his brain trying to find a way to do it.

Knowing how important this was had been the only reason he'd stepped away from Mery. He'd left him with Qebui, Jimmy, and Iah, who seemed to have forgiven him for leaving and not talking to him for a while. Mery wouldn't be any safer than he was with two gods, no matter how minor they were.

Sed stared at the door in front of him. He was at the wing of the celestial palace Isis and Osiris shared. He'd tried knocking already, but the only result he'd gotten was that someone had opened the door, taken one look at him, and told him Isis wasn't seeing anyone before slamming the door shut again.

Mery wasn't expecting Sed for a while, so Sed decided to visit Nu. There was no one more powerful than them, not even Ra. If Sed managed to get them to intervene, everything would be fine.

He made his way toward Nu's wing. The celestial palace was huge, and while Sed could easily have moved from one wing to another using his powers, he wanted to walk for a bit. He needed time to think and come up with a way to get Nu interested in Mery's fate so they would help.

He hadn't found anything by the time he reached their door. He hesitated once he was there. He doubted they would be angry at seeing him, but it didn't mean they would be happy, either. Usually, no one disturbed them, especially not in their rooms. But Nu had been there after the coronation ceremony, and they'd seemed to like Mery. Sed had to focus on that and hope it would be enough.

The door swung open before he could knock. Nu stood in front of him, smiling. Today, they were wearing sweatpants and a t-shirt. It was startling, but it made Sed smile.

"My favorite grandson. To what do I owe this pleasure?" Nu asked.

"I didn't know I was your favorite grandson." They had hundreds of them, so it was surprising.

Nu waved them in. "You always were one of my favorites. You have your head on your shoulders, and you've never acted foolishly like most of my children and grandchildren have. Now come in and tell me what brought you here."

Sed obeyed and stepped into the room. It was wide, with enormous windows that allowed the breeze and the sun to come in. Nu made a beeline for a table on the terrace, and when Sed followed them, he saw a man was sitting there. He didn't think he'd ever met the guy, but one glance was enough to tell him the man wasn't part of the Egyptian pantheon. His hair was long and black, and his skin was so pale it was almost translucent. He was wearing a black t-shirt and black leather pants, and he seemed amused when he noticed Sed was staring.

The man couldn't be human, since no human had ever visited the celestial palace. That meant he was a god, but which one?

"Sit with us," Nu said.

Sed cautiously sat in one of the empty chairs. He was still staring at the man, but he was distracted when something

wound around his ankles. He looked down to see a mummi-
fied cat rubbing its face against his leg.

"Don't mind Miu. He's always liked people," Nu said.
They took a sip from a cup sitting on the table in front of them.
"And we don't get near enough visits anymore."

Sed reached down and scratched the top of the cat's head.
That meant he was scratching bandages, but the cat didn't
seem to care.

"Are you ready to tell us why you're here?" Nu asked.

Sed moved his attention back to them and the man. "I'd
like to talk to you about what's going on with Mery and the
prime minister."

Nu smiled. "That's why Loki is here, too. I didn't know the
two of you knew each other."

Sed gaped. "We don't." He'd had no idea this man was
Loki.

"I see. I was surprised to see him on my doorstep, as I was
surprised to see you, but I'm glad both of you visited me. Loki
was telling me someone attacked the king?"

Sed swallowed. "Maybe Mery and the others should be
here when we talk about this." It was dangerous to ask, but if
there was anyone who might agree to that, it was Nu. After
all, they were having tea with a god from another pantheon
in their rooms in the celestial palace. No human had ever visited, but Sed suspected no god from another pantheon had,
either, until today.

"I don't see why not," Nu said. "I'd like to meet your king."

"You were at the party after his coronation ceremony."

"I was, but I didn't talk to him. He was uncomfortable, and
when the two of you disappeared, I decided to give you time
alone. Now seems like it's time for us to meet, though. After
all, I have to make sure he's worthy of you."

That wasn't what Sed had expected, but Nu would get
whatever they wanted, and if Sed wished to have their help,

he had to go along with this. Besides, he kind of liked the idea of Mery getting to know Nu. Sed might not be close to his grandparent, but that didn't mean he didn't love them. He wanted Mery to meet his family, not only his mother and his cousin but everyone else, too.

It might just be the first step to that happening.

Mery smiled when Sed walked into the office. He was happy for the distraction, even though he knew it would only last a few minutes. He couldn't afford to take more time off, especially not when he and Jimmy were working to find a way to replace the prime minister.

There was something in Sed's expression that made Mery pause. He narrowed his eyes, trying to read him, but he couldn't. "What happened?" he asked.

Sed rubbed the back of his neck. "None of the big five agreed to talk to me."

Mery hadn't realized Sed was going to the celestial palace. He wasn't surprised about the news, though. Why would powerful gods care about him? They might want him to be their messenger, but it could easily be someone else. It didn't even have to be someone who descended from the old pharaohs. But even if it did, Mery had a brother. Mery never wanted him to come close to the throne, but he supposed gods wouldn't care about that.

"What now?" Qebui asked, leaning back in his chair.

He looked tired, which Mery was surprised to see. He hadn't thought gods could feel tired, although of course, he didn't know much about most of them. Sed slept and shared his bed, so maybe Mery should have realized they were just like humans—with weird powers.

"I didn't know Loki had agreed to help," Sed said instead of answering Qebui's question.

It got Qebui's attention, and he straightened in his chair. "How do you know?"

"I decided to visit Nu since I was there. Imagine my surprise when I walked into their rooms and found Loki sitting with them discussing the problem."

Qebui looked shocked for a moment. "The asshole didn't even call to tell me he was here," he complained.

"You shouldn't have pulled him in. He doesn't belong to our pantheon. His presence is probably going to make things even harder."

"Or it could make things easier. He cares, while our gods don't. I just want Mery to be safe and happy. I know you want the same. Do you really care how we manage that?"

Sed sighed. "I don't," he said. "Nu wants to see the four of us."

Mery's eyes widened. "What do you mean?" he asked.

Sed turned his attention to him. "Exactly that. I told them I needed their help, and they want to hear the story, but I thought it would be better if you were there, too."

"Are they coming here?" Mery looked around. The office was a bit of a mess, but he supposed he and Jimmy could clean up easily.

Sed shook his head. "We're going there. It's already bad enough that Loki is at the celestial palace. Can you imagine what would happen if he appeared *here?*"

Too easily, and Mery almost *wanted* it to happen. Maybe it would shock the prime minister into having a heart attack or something like that. Mery didn't want the prime minister to die, but having him out of the way would make things easier for everyone, especially him.

"Didn't you say there's never been a human in the celestial palace?" Jimmy asked.

He was holding his arm close to his chest, probably still in pain from being stabbed. Mery had tried sending him back to his rooms to rest, but Jimmy had glared at him and told him he was okay. Mery could tell he wasn't, but he was glad to have Jimmy by his side.

"Not as far as I know, but today will be a day for firsts. Are you willing to go?"

Mery shot to his feet. "I'm ready," he said.

That appeared to strike Sed as funny, but Mery didn't care. He would be taking time away from work, but he would be in a place where he felt safe, or at least safer than he was here, and he would see a place no other human had ever seen. Why was Sed even asking?

Mery and Jimmy stood waiting.

Sed took Mery's hand while Qebui took care of Jimmy, wrapping an arm around his shoulders. Jimmy briefly leaned against him, and when he noticed Mery watching them, he blushed.

Mery could only smile. He wanted Jimmy to be happy, and if that was with Qebui, he had nothing to say about it. He hadn't been sure about the god in the beginning, but he'd revealed himself to be a friend.

One second, they were standing in the office. The next, they were in a palace Mery had never seen, and his knees almost buckled under him.

Everywhere he looked, things were white and golden and so clean Mery could probably have eaten off the floor. It was much bigger than the human palace he lived in, but there was no one around, which was strange after seeing servants and guards everywhere. Mery looked around, not knowing what to expect, but this place looked pretty much like a human palace, only bigger. That was a bit disappointing, but Sed didn't give him time to say anything about it. Never releasing his hand, he pulled him toward a door to their right. He quickly knocked. Then, when a voice answered, he pulled Mery inside.

These rooms were much more colorful than the hallway had been. There was still a lot of white, but whoever lived here had put their own touches to the place. There were colors everywhere, too, and just the sight of the red blanket on the couch and the green rug next to the coffee table helped Mery relax.

Mery tensed again when Sed led him to a terrace and he saw two people sitting around the table. They were eating, but one of them got to their feet when they saw Mery and the others. Mery had no doubt they were facing Nu, which meant the man who was still sitting was Loki. Mery wondered how the god wasn't too hot with his leather pants and black t-shirt, but he wasn't about to ask.

"This is Meryatum, the new pharaoh," Sed explained. "Mery, this is Nu."

Mery bowed. His eyes widened when he saw a cat coming toward him, or at least, he thought it was a cat. It was bandaged like a mummy. Mery looked at Sed, not knowing what to do, but Sed smiled and shrugged.

"It's a pleasure to meet you," Nu said. "My grandson told me you're having a bit of trouble?"

Mery chuckled. "You could call it that, I suppose. One of my best friends was stabbed trying to protect me, so for me, it's more than a *bit* of trouble."

"Why don't we all sit down and talk about it?"

They did. Mery relaxed as the time passed and the gods around the table behaved normally. He didn't know what he'd expected, but it wasn't this. This was better, and he was relieved Nu wasn't asking personal questions about his relationship with Sed. Mery would have answered, but they didn't seem to doubt that Mery was the best person for Sed to be with.

Once they knew everything, Nu tapped their fingertip against their chin. "You *are* in a bit of a pickle," they said.

139

Mery blinked. He wasn't sure what that meant, but he could guess.

"I could kill them," Loki offered.

It was the first time he spoke, and Mery hoped he wasn't going to take things into his own hands and kill Anhur and the prime minister. Was it even possible for him to kill a god? He sounded convinced, but it didn't mean he could do it.

"Don't be an idiot," Qebui told him. "You can't kill a god, especially not one from another pantheon."

Loki pouted. "That's not fair. Why did you make me come if I can't even kill anyone?"

"I didn't *make* you come. I told you I was having trouble, and you decided to come by without even telling me. I had to find out you were here through my cousin. I'll remember that, by the way."

"I was going to visit you. I've been friends with Nu a lot longer than I've been friends with you, though, so I thought it was better if I stopped here first."

"We should focus on the important thing here," Sed intervened. "Nu, I know you don't like to be involved in what happens in the human world. I would never ask you to be if it wasn't important."

Nu looked from Sed to Mery. To Mery's surprise, they pushed a bowl of strawberries closer to him and clucked their tongue. "You're too thin. You should eat more."

Mery grabbed a strawberry and stuffed it in his mouth. When the parent of all Egyptian gods—god from whom the world originated—told you to eat, you ate.

Nu looked satisfied. "I apologize for what my grandchildren have been doing to you," they said. "You look like a sweet boy, and I want you and Sed to be happy. I'm still not entirely sure we truly need a king and a messenger, but I understand you can't back out of the position, and I admire you for not doing it, especially after you were attacked."

Mery tried hard not to hope. If Nu intervened, everything would be okay. They were the most powerful god Mery knew about, even more powerful than the big five.

"Does that mean you'll help him?" Sed asked.

Nu stared for a moment. Then, slowly, they nodded. "I'll help. The way my grandchildren are behaving is atrocious, and I'm ashamed of them. I also don't want anything to happen to your Mery."

Mery relaxed. With one sentence, Nu had agreed to help and had given their approval to his and Sed's relationship. Mery didn't care what happened next. He knew things would be okay, and that was enough.

CHAPTER TEN

Sed wasn't sure why Nu had asked him and Mery to visit again, but he hoped it had something to do with the promise they'd made to keep Mery safe. Even after they had, Sed had trouble sleeping. He kept waking up at the slightest sound, thinking someone had come to kill Mery. It hadn't happened so far, but the prime minister was still working and plotting, and Sed doubted he would wait much longer to strike again.

Qebui and Jimmy were all mysterious about something they were working on when it came to the prime minister. No matter how many times Sed and Mery asked, they brushed them off, telling them to focus on running the country. It was both a relief and worrying. Sed wanted to know what was going on, but he couldn't deny that he and Mery had a lot of work to do, and not having to worry about the prime minister helped. It gave them time to focus on everything else, which was sorely needed.

"I still can't get over how pretty this place is," Mery murmured.

Just like last time, Sed had appeared them in front of the door of Nu's rooms. Mery was more relaxed now, and Sed knew it had a lot to do with the way Nu had accepted him. They hadn't said anything about Sed and Mery being together. If anything, they'd seemed to approve, which he knew Mery was happy with. Sed was, too. He didn't need his grandparent's approval to be with Mery, but it felt good to have it.

He raised his hand and knocked on the door. It opened only a few moments later, and Sed grinned when he saw what Nu was wearing. "I don't think I've ever seen you in a pair of jeans," he told them as he and Mery walked in.

Nu turned around to look at their ass. "I like the way they make my legs look."

That wasn't something Sed wanted to think about, but if Nu was happy, so was he. "You wanted to see us?" he asked.

Nu looked at them again. "I did. Let's go on the terrace."

Sed wasn't surprised. The terrace seemed to be Nu's favorite place, and Sed didn't blame them. It was beautiful, and since they were in the celestial palace, it wasn't too hot, even though it was in full sun.

Sed froze as soon as his feet were on the terrace. He stared at Anhur, who was sitting at the table in the seat Loki had occupied when he'd visited — which thankfully hadn't been for more than a few hours and without spilled blood. Anhur looked smug for all of a second before saw Sed and Mery. Then he shot to his feet, looking from them to Nu.

"What's the meaning of this?" he asked.

Nu's expression hardened. "You tell me."

"I have to go," Anhur said.

He moved toward the door that would lead him inside the palace, but Nu placed themself in front of him. "You'll sit your ass back in the chair and listen to what I have to say," they snapped.

Sed wasn't used to hearing them talk that way, and he was glad their anger wasn't aimed at him. He never wanted to do anything to anger them. No one knew exactly how powerful they were, but they were the creator of all gods and humans. Sed suspected they could destroy them as easily as they'd created them.

Anhur sat, but he looked nervous now. He kept peeking at Mery, who was glaring at him.

143

"So," Nu said once everyone was sitting around the table. "Sed told me what you've been up to," they told Anhur.

"I haven't been doing anything. I enjoy visiting the human world. So does he, and I don't see anyone having a problem with that."

Nu's eyes narrowed. "Do you think I'm an idiot?"

"Of course not. I apologize if that's the impression I gave you."

"I don't care about your apologies. I don't think Mery does, either. I don't even care about why you've been plotting with the prime minister to kill Mery. It stops, and it stops *now*."

"You can't order me to—"

Nu sat up straighter. "I can order you to do anything I want. You should remember who I am and what I could do to you."

"I remember," Anhur said. "But—"

"No *buts*. This is disgraceful. I don't care how involved you are with humans. We're gods, and we're always going to be involved with them, willing or not. I won't allow you to hurt Mery, though, especially not now that he's with Sed. You *will* leave them alone if you don't want to be locked in your rooms here in the palace." Nu paused. "And If you don't want to take a walk in the underworld. Osiris wouldn't refuse me this favor."

Sed didn't think he would, even though he'd refused to talk to Sed. All of the big five had, and he hoped Nu would talk to them, too. They might be gods, and they might be powerful, but it didn't mean they could afford to stay away from what the other gods did. In a way, all gods were related to each other. The big five should have stepped in because it was the right thing to do instead of ignoring the problem.

It was easy to imagine what would have happened if Nu had stayed out of the situation. Mery would have eventually ended up dead, and that wasn't something Sed wanted to think about.

"Do you understand me?" Nu asked softly.

Anhur nodded. "I understand, and I'll stay in my rooms here in the palace for a while."

"Good. I also want the names of the people you've been working with, be they humans or gods."

Anhur's eyes widened. "Will you hurt them?"

"I'll punish them. I don't appreciate the way you and some of my grandchildren have been acting. You're behaving like savages, and I should know, since I *created* savages. I think it's time for me to stop isolating myself so much and step back into the world. It clearly needs it."

Anhur looked like he wanted to run away, but he clearly knew better than to try leaving before Nu gave permission. He kept glaring at Sed and Mery.

Sed didn't care. He didn't think Anhur would go against a direct order, especially not coming from Nu. They wouldn't hesitate to chuck him into the underworld if he did.

"Now, give me those names," Nu said. "I'll make sure they can't hurt Mery. You won't ever see those people again, and they'll regret ever associating with you. I won't hurt them, but I need to make sure this doesn't happen again."

Sed was so relieved he could have kissed them. He hadn't known what to expect when he'd visited them, but it wasn't this.

For as long as Sed could remember, Nu had always kept themself separate. He could understand why. They'd seen and created so much that they deserved whatever they wanted, even if it was time away from humans and gods alike. He was relieved they had agreed to intervene, and even more that they'd decided it was time for them to stop hiding in the celestial palace.

If there was one person who could work miracles, it was Nu.

After giving them the list of humans he was working with, Anhur scurried away with his tail between his legs. If it was up to him, this would have been resolved through a fight to the death or something like that, but Nu wouldn't allow that to happen. They'd spoken, and everyone had to obey.

"Thank you," Mery murmured.

Nu reached over the table to pat his hand. "You don't have to thank me. I was more than happy to do this for you and Sed. He's always been one of my favorite grandchildren." They winked at Sed. "And I'll make sure nothing happens to you. It's time for me to come out of retirement."

"I'm sorry you have to," Mery told them.

"I'm not. I've been staying away for a long time, and I feel like I missed a lot of things, including how awful my children and grandchildren's behavior has been. It's time to put an end to that."

Sed had no doubt they would. They were a force of nature, and even the big five would have to kneel in front of them.

That wasn't what Sed had been planning or had thought would happen, but it wasn't a bad thing. Maybe it was time to make sure gods stopped hurting humans just because they could. He couldn't think of a better person to help do that than Nu.

Mery was in shock by the time he and Sed appeared back in his office. "Did that really happen?" he asked.

Before Sed could answer, Nu appeared next to them. They looked around, then nodded. "This will do. Mery, I'd like a suite of rooms next to yours. I'm sure Sed's old rooms will do."

Mery didn't ask how they knew Sed had a suite of rooms next to his or that Sed had barely spent time in it since they'd gotten together. "I'll have someone clean it up." If Sed didn't want to move in with him officially, they could find him a guest room somewhere.

"And I'll move my things," Sed added. "It's not like I've been spending time there anyway."

"What will the two of you do now?" Nu asked.

"They're planning to deal with the prime minister," Qebui said. "With my help."

Jimmy and Qebui were sitting at a table, but they'd both risen to their feet when Mery, Sed, and Nu had appeared. They looked excited, and Mery couldn't wait to find out what they'd come up with.

Nu smiled. "Good. I hope the palace will be peaceful by the time I get back."

They disappeared again, and Mery turned his attention to Qebui and Jimmy. "What did you find?"

"Enough to have him arrested if you want," Qebui said. "Sometimes, it pays to be the god of the North winds. People don't notice when there's a breeze, and I've been moving around the palace for days collecting proof and getting everything together. I have documents that show he was plotting to push you off the throne as soon as he could. I have other documents that prove he was behind the attempted assassination, including a declaration from his niece. He's done."

"What about the other ministers?"

"They won't be able to deny he was involved. Besides, a few of their names are on those documents, too. Unfortunately for you, you'll have to find new ministers, and soon. It's better for you to get rid of the rats, though. I don't think you want someone who wishes you harm working with you."

Mery didn't, but this was going to be a headache. He sighed and rubbed his forehead. "I don't, but I wish I didn't have to do this." He looked at Qebui. "Is there any chance I can convince you to become prime minister?"

Qebui snorted. "I'm your friend, but I have no intention of

having anything to do with your job."

Mery didn't point out that Qebui had already involved himself. He was relieved and grateful he hadn't had to face all of this on his own. He suspected the prime minister would have eventually succeeded in getting rid of him if that had been the case.

"All right. I want to see the prime minister."

Jimmy beamed and got to work. Mery had no doubt Ouser would try to find a way out of this meeting, but eventually, he would come. When the king called for you, it was the only thing you could do, especially when you were the prime minister.

Still, it took Ouser almost an hour to knock on Mery's door. By that time, Mery was so angry he was tempted to throw the man into the dungeons without even talking to him. Not that they had dungeons, but Mery was tempted to create one just for the prime minister.

"Your majesty," Ouser said as he walked in. He bowed slightly, just enough to be able to say he'd bowed, but not enough for it to be a sign of respect.

Mery didn't care. At this point, he didn't care about what the prime minister thought of him or what he'd been planning. He just wanted the man out of his life.

He faced the prime minister with Qebui and Sed by his side. There was a pile of paper on his desk, which Jimmy had told him was the proof he needed to deal with the prime minister. He didn't take it yet, wanting to see what Ouser had to say.

"I just had an audience with Nu," Mery began.

Ouser's eyes widened for a moment before he schooled his expression. "The primordial god?"

"Them. They were informed that some of their grandchildren were involving themselves in my reign. They didn't like it, and unfortunately for you, Anhur was punished."

"Anhur?" the prime minister asked. He'd started sweating, and while it was hot in the room, Mery suspected it had more to do with how nervous and scared he was than with the weather.

"Your associate. And don't bother trying to deny it. I heard the two of you talking. I know you were plotting against me for the throne."

"I'm the prime minister. I don't need the throne."

"Maybe not, but it would have been good for you to be seen as the gods' messenger. If I'd married your niece and had given her a child before mysteriously dying, you wouldn't have hesitated to take my place on the throne until my child was old enough."

"It would have taken years, your majesty. I don't think anyone would plot that kind of thing."

"I agree with you. A lot of people would be unhappy with how long it would take, which is why you kept me in the dark when it comes to my role and duties as king. You made sure that I had nothing to do with guiding the country. I'm not an idiot, Ouser. It didn't take me long to realize what you are doing, and while I didn't want to believe it, and it sometimes made sense for me not to be involved in how the country is ruled, it's over. It might take me years, but I'll learn how to be a good king, and I'll learn without you."

"You can't fire me," the prime minister protested.

"I can do what I want. I'm the king. Besides, I'm not firing you as much as arresting you." Mery gestured at the documents on his desk. "I have proof of what you did. Now, you can decide how to react. You'll get arrested either way, but if you go graciously, it won't be a scandal. Your family might manage to stay out of it. If you try anything, though, I'll make sure you're arrested publicly." Mery paused a moment to let his words sink in. Then, he added, "And don't think your minister friends will be able to do anything for you. They'll be arrested and fired, too. It's over, Ouser. We could have worked together, but instead, you decided to go against me, and you lost."

In a way, Mery was sorry to lose Ouser. As far as he could see, the man had once been a decent prime minister. He'd allowed greed and the need for power to take over, and he'd ruined everything. Mery had no idea who he would replace the man with, but he was going to have to come up with a name, and soon. First, though, he would talk to the ministers who remained in their place. They might have an idea of who he could trust.

Two guards had to drag the former prime minister away. Even though Mery had warned him to go along with it, Ouser did anything but. He continued threatening Mery until Mery and the others couldn't hear him anymore. The guards were alarmed, but Mery waved them away and closed the office door behind them. He leaned against it, gazing at the people who were still in the office with him.

He trusted all three of them with his life. He looked at Qebui, who arched a brow at him and shook his head. "No matter what you say, I'm *not* saying yes to being your prime minister. Actually, Jimmy and I have something to do."

"I wasn't thinking of asking you again," Mery protested, but it was too late. Qebui had already grabbed Jimmy's hand and had disappeared, taking him with him.

Mery couldn't help but smile. He couldn't force his friends to do anything, and he couldn't fill all the jobs with people he trusted the way he trusted these three. It was enough for him that Jimmy was his personal assistant. Together, the four of them would be able to come up with names and replace Ouser and the ministers that had worked against Mery.

Sed wrapped an arm around Mery's shoulders and kissed his temple. "You were great," he murmured.

"I wish I hadn't had to do this. Who am I going to choose

as prime minister now?"

"I don't know, but you won't have to choose by yourself. I'm not going anywhere, and neither are Qebui and Jimmy. And of course, if you want, I'm sure Nu will help you."

And who better to help Mery guide the country than the god who had created the people and gods who inhabited it?

EPILOGUE

Sed was going to have to make it official. He knew that was what everyone expected. After all, he was already the king's consort, albeit unofficially. He was also Mery's closest advisor, along with Qebui and Jimmy.

A lot of people didn't like it. Jimmy was a foreigner, and he shouldn't have a place so close to the king. Sed and Qebui were gods, and they didn't belong with humans. No one had said anything to them, though. They wouldn't dare, especially not with Nu living in the palace and acting as if Mery and Jimmy were their grandsons. Some days, Sed wondered if Nu liked them more than they liked him and Qebui.

He didn't resent it. Jimmy barely had a family, and while Mery had his mother, he didn't have grandparents. Nu had slipped into the role with an eagerness that surprised Sed. They didn't usually have any kind of contact with humans, but they obviously had decided to change that. Sed was happy to see how they were with Jimmy and Mery, even though they continued pushing him to marry Mery, or at the very least, to propose.

And maybe he would. He'd been waiting for the perfect time, but he was starting to suspect there would be no perfect time. His and Mery's lives were frantic and full of people and things to do, and it was hard to find time alone. Besides, Sed wasn't sure Mery would say yes. He knew he ought to get married since he was the king, but so far, he hadn't said anything about it to Sed. It wasn't like Sed could give him children anyway.

"What are you thinking about so hard?" Nu asked as they poked Sed in the ribs.

He twisted to avoid their fingers. "Nothing."

"I don't believe that." They took a piece of watermelon from their plate and stared at Sed with narrowed eyes. "Did Mery finally decide to make an honest god out of you?"

Mery, who had been taking a sip of coffee, spluttered and almost showered Qebui with it. Loki the dog, who had been sitting at Mery's feet, jumped up and barked as if he expected someone to attack his new master. He'd been protective of Mery for a while, and Sed liked to imagine the dog understood how important Mery was to him.

Nu looked from Mery to Sed. "No?" They sounded disappointed.

"Mery is young to be married."

"But not young enough *not* to get married," Jimmy pointed out. "And you know, I checked the laws. There are a few things to fix, but there's nothing that says he can't marry a god."

"We never talked about marriage," Mery said. He was staring at Sed, but when he saw Sed had noticed, he looked away.

"What is there to talk about?" Nu asked. "You love him, and he loves you. He's your closest advisor, and he's already acting like your consort. Don't you want to marry him?"

Mery hesitated.

Sed held his breath—they'd never talked about that. It was implied that eventually they would have to get married, since they were together and Mery was the king. It would make things easier when it came to dealing with other countries, but also with their own. Some people might not be happy their king was dating a god, but the wedding might smooth things out. It also might not, so Sed wasn't holding his breath.

He couldn't say he had anything against marrying Mery. Actually, he kind of wanted to. He'd never imagined himself getting married to anyone, least of all a human king, but now that he had Mery in his life, he couldn't think of not having him. If it took them getting married to be sure Mery wouldn't be taken away from him, Sed was ready to do just that.

He wanted to make Mery happy. He was doing his best every day, but it was clear they didn't know each other well enough yet and that they needed to talk.

"We'll do it at our own pace," Mery said. He got to his feet. "Now, if you'll excuse me, I have work to do."

He walked away. Sed watched him go until Nu elbowed him in the side. "Go after him and propose."

"You don't know he'll say yes." Sed wanted to puke at the thought he might not.

Nu rolled their eyes. "He loves you, and he wants to be with you. Why would he say no? But you won't find out until you ask, and you better do it now before I start organizing everything. I thought an autumn wedding would be nice."

Sed got to his feet as Qebui snickered. It didn't last long because Nu turned their attention to him, pointing a finger at him. "Don't laugh, because you and Jimmy are next. I'll see both you and Sed married before I decide it's time for me to go back to the celestial palace."

Qebui paled, and Sed walked away laughing.

He found Mery in his office, already sitting behind his desk. Mery initially tensed, but when he saw it was Sed, he relaxed and smiled. "You didn't have to follow me. I'm sure you want time with your family."

"You're my family. If you're here, this is where I'll spend time."

Mery looked away, but he was still smiling. "You don't have to marry me just because Nu said so."

"How about I marry you because I want to?"

Mery got to his feet and moved closer. "Do you? Because I know I'm human and that eventually I'll die. I don't want you to have to go through that."

"The only way I wouldn't is if I were dating a god, and that's not happening anytime soon." Sed hesitated. He hadn't looked into this yet, which was why he hadn't mentioned it to Mery, but now, he couldn't avoid it. "What if you could become immortal?"

Mery froze. He stared at Sed with wide eyes and licked his lips. "What are you talking about?"

"I'm a god. More importantly, Nu is a god, and I'm their favorite grandchild. I'm pretty sure they would give me anything I asked, especially when it comes to you."

"Are you saying they could make me immortal?"

"Many gods could. They don't usually do it because they view humans as unimportant. I don't, though, and neither does Nu. I don't want you to say yes just because you think you have to. It's just something to keep in mind, especially if you're worried about me losing you."

Sed wasn't surprised when Mery threw himself into his arms. He'd expected it. Even though Mery appeared steady and calm in official settings, he was anything but when they were alone. When they were, Mery was loving and exuberant, and he never missed a chance to show that to Sed.

"Does that mean you want to marry me?" Sed asked, closing his arms around Mery.

Mery looked up and kissed him. "I do. I wish we could wait until we're both ready, but I realize it's complicated. Besides, I don't think that waiting will change anything. I love you."

Sed couldn't stop the smile that bloomed on his lips. "I love you, too." They kissed again. Then Sed asked, "Marry me?"

"Yes."

Sed might have lost the life he'd wanted when he'd moved to the United States, but he didn't regret anything. In its place, he had gained so much that some days, he could barely believe it. He had Mery, of course, with all the complications and happiness that came with him. He still had Jimmy, who had been the most important person in his past life. He had Nu, Qebui, and Iah, who were part of his life again and who he wasn't planning on losing ever again. He even had his mother back, although he wasn't quite sure how to feel about that yet

Even though in the beginning, coming here had felt like he'd be able to extricate himself from the situation as soon as he wanted, it had been inescapable. Just like Mery couldn't pull away from being king, Sed couldn't pull away from loving him or being who he was — Sed, the protector of kingship, consort to the king, friend and family to Jimmy, Nu, Qebui, and Iah.

And he didn't want to.

You may also enjoy the following from eXtasy Books Inc:

Not Ordinary
Catherine Lievens

Excerpt

Jarvis didn't know what to think of Peregrine's request. It didn't make sense. Even if Peregrine were a bother, he was friends with Sam and the others. Jarvis was sure they would find a way to show him around without taking time away from their jobs and studies.

And even if they couldn't, why was Peregrine asking him of all people to show him around town and pack territory? Anyone would have been better. Even Jarvis's siblings would have been better. He didn't know how old Peregrine was, but he had to be older than Jarvis, maybe around the age of Jarvis's brother Todd. It would make more sense for them to spend time together than it would for Jarvis and Peregrine.

But Peregrine had asked so gently and nicely that Jarvis couldn't say no. He had no idea what would happen, but he would find out soon enough. It wasn't like Peregrine had asked him to become his best friend anyway. He just needed help to find his bearings, and once that was done, Jarvis doubted they would ever talk again.

His shift had never felt so long. He kept watching the clock, then peeking at Peregrine, wondering if he was bored. He didn't seem to be. He'd grabbed one of the books the coffee shop owner kept on the shelves against the walls, and he was reading. He looked up a few times and noticed Jarvis was staring at him, but he limited himself to smiling and going back to the book.

Jarvis still didn't know what to think by the time his shift was over, but he was relieved anyway. He went to the backroom to put down his apron and grab his backpack, but before going back to Peregrine, he got him another coffee. Even if he wasn't done drinking the last one he'd gotten, it was cold by now.

Jarvis walked over to Peregrine, still watching him. Peregrine was so engrossed in his book that he didn't realize Jarvis was there until Jarvis stood right next to him.

"I'm done," Jarvis said.

Peregrine jerked. His elbow knocked against Jarvis's arm, and Jarvis dropped the coffee. He scrambled back as it splashed all over the floor. He and Peregrine stared at it, then they moved at the same time, both of them reaching down to clean up. Jarvis didn't have the time to move back when he realized what was about to happen, and his forehead hit Peregrine's. At the same time, he smelled the one thing he'd never thought he'd smell — his mate. He couldn't think about that right now, and he wasn't ready to believe the scent came from the mn in front of him. It just wasn't possible.

Jarvis jerked back, holding a hand to his head. It hurt, but he didn't care. He wanted to make sure he hadn't hurt Peregrine.

"I'm sorry," he said. He should have known he would make a disaster. He always did. "Are you hurt? Do you need ice?"

To Jarvis's surprise, Peregrine started laughing. "I'm fine," he said between two snickers. "We're disasters, though, aren't we?"

Jarvis found himself smiling. Maybe he'd been wrong and Peregrine wasn't his mate. Peregrine hadn't said anything, and he'd have smelled Jarvis since Jarvis had smelled him. "I don't know about you, but this is pretty normal for me." He looked at the floor. "I'm going to grab the mop and clean this up. We can go right after I'm done, or maybe you want to go home? I wouldn't blame you since I just head-butted you."

Peregrine shook his head. "I'm not going anywhere, and I'll help you clean up."

Jarvis stared. He'd expected Peregrine to have enough of him already, but instead, he was still smiling. What the fuck was going on? This wasn't Jarvis's life. He didn't have friends, and he didn't make people laugh, except when he fell on his face.

"You don't have to help me," Jarvis said.

"I don't mind. It was my fault, after all."

"I shouldn't have startled you."

"It's fine," Peregrine said. "You grab the mop. I'll throw away the mug and use napkins to get a start."

Jarvis couldn't leave a mess, so he headed back to the backroom. By the time he was back with Peregrine, most of the coffee wasn't on the floor anymore. Peregrine had dragged one of the trash cans closer, and he'd dumped all the wet napkins he'd used and the now empty travel mug into it. He smiled when he heard Jarvis come closer, and Jarvis couldn't help but ask, "Why me?" Because if they weren't mates, it didn't make sense.

Peregrine frowned. "I'm not sure what you're asking."

"I know you said you didn't want to be a bother to the others, but I'm sure they wouldn't mind. And even if they did, why did you ask me to show you around? I'm sure pretty much anyone else in the pack would have been better."

Peregrine stared at Jarvis, so much so that Jarvis started cleaning the floor just to do something. He could feel Peregrine's gaze on his face, and it was heavy and incomprehensible.

"I don't know about you, but I don't have friends," Peregrine finally said.

Jarvis barked out a laugh. "If you want to know how to make friends, I'm the wrong person to ask. I don't have friends, either."

Peregrine frowned. "I don't understand why. You're a nice person."

"You don't know me. But you've seen what a disaster I am already. It makes sense that no one wants to spend time with me."

Peregrine shook his head. "It doesn't. You dropped a coffee. No one died, and nothing bad happened. I don't understand why you're so negative about yourself, but I suppose I'll find out once we're friends."

Jarvis didn't want Peregrine to find out anything. He doubted Peregrine would want to spend any amount of time with him once he did, but he couldn't find it in himself to say that he didn't want to see Peregrine again. It would be a lie. He wanted to spend time with Peregrine and get to know him.

It wasn't only because Peregrine was a rare shifter, because he was a healer, or even because he was gorgeous. There was something about him, something gentle and nice, that attracted Jarvis more than everything else put together. He still didn't understand how Peregrine thought or why he'd asked him of all people to be friends, but until Peregrine decided otherwise, Jarvis wasn't going anywhere.

Maybe they were mates after all. Gosh, this was so confusing.

"Unless you'd rather not be friends with me?" Peregrine asked. There was pain in his voice, but also resignation. "I'd understand. I realize I'm weird, and being friends with me is probably dangerous. Some people would do a lot to get their hands on me because of what I can do. It would be safer for you to stay away from me."

Was that why Peregrine didn't have friends? Because no one wanted to be close to him when people might try to kidnap him? Jarvis found himself angry at the thought. People should be grateful for Peregrine's presence in their life. It didn't have anything to do with him being a healer, but everything with him being a good person. It would be easy for Peregrine to decide he never wanted to heal anyone again so he could stay out of trouble. Instead, he'd helped Basil, and he'd almost been captured because of it.

"I want to be your friend," Jarvis said, sounding more convinced than he was. This was what Peregrine needed, and Jarvis wanted to give it to him.

"Are you sure?" Peregrine sounded hesitant. "Because I would understand if it were better for you to stay away from me. You don't have to say yes to being my friend just because I asked."

Jarvis put the mop back into the bucket and looked right at Peregrine, something he'd avoided doing until now. "I don't want to be your friend just because you asked. I've wanted to get to know you since you arrived in Rosewood, so this is perfect."

"Why do you want to get to know me?"

Jarvis shrugged. He didn't know how to answer that without sounding like a creep. "Why do you want to get to know me?"

Peregrine stared for a moment. Then, he smiled. "I suppose you're right. Friends, then?"

Jarvis couldn't believe this, but he found himself nodding anyway. "Friends," he confirmed.

"For now," Peregrine added.

Jarvis licked his lips. "What does that mean?"

Peregrine's lips curled. "We'll have to talk about the fact that we're mates eventually, but for now, this is fine."

Jarvis swallowed. He hadn't been wrong after all.

ABOUT THE AUTHOR

Catherine is the creator of several series, most of them paranormal, including the Whitedell Pride Series and the Gillham Pack Series. While she graduated in translation, she decided to go the writer's way because it was more fun to create her own stories and characters.

She's been living in Italy for more than twenty years, but she's a daughter of the North—Belgium to be precise—and she misses it so much that she's already planning to move back.

She loves pizza—probably too much—her son, her pets, and of course, books. She sneaks some reading time into her schedule every time she has five minutes free from writing, demands from her various pets and son, and lastly, housework.

Connect with her:

lievens.catherine@gmail.com
BookBub: https://www.bookbub.com/authors/catherine-lievens
Website: https://authorcatherinelievens.com/
Facebook: https://www.facebook.com/catherine.lievens.9
Facebook Group: https://www.facebook.com/groups/411788002341528/
Twitter: https://twitter.com/authorCLievens
Newsletter: http://eepurl.com/c-uvKn